MAN CAVE

ON A MANHUNT
BOOK 3

VANESSA VALE

Life's not simple. Neither is love.

I'm twenty-four, and ahem... inexperienced.
When a blind date doesn't change that status, Theo
volunteers for the task.
Who's Theo? Just the guy I've been crushing on for six
months. Yeah, him. Tall, broad and handsome and gah,
now he's even got a beard!
He's diligent. Very focused. Skilled. And impossible not to
fall for.
Except he's only up for a fun time. A wild romp or two.
No way would he have any romantic interest in someone
like me. Why would he? He's an intense, brooding doctor—
and, oh yeah, a billionaire—and I'm a goofy first grade
teacher barely making ends meet.
When my goal changes from man-made O's to the man
himself, I know I'm in trouble.
Because he's no longer a crush, but someone I might
actually love.

*With all the books in the On A Manhunt series, it's always open
season on men.*

1

THEO

I'D BEEN at the job three hours and I was already having second thoughts. Not about Hunter Valley. The town was cool as shit. I'd visited before since Maverick pretty much moved his ass up here because of a work project... then a woman project. And Dex, who had a Hunter Valley woman project of his own but was settled in Denver with her.

There wasn't a woman messing with my life.

I'd done that all by myself. Maybe I should have visited Family Health Services before I quit being a trauma surgeon and accepted the role as family physician. Over the phone. It was like buying a boat sight unseen only to arrive at the marina and discover it was barely afloat.

The medical practice wasn't sinking. I was.

Over the weekend, I'd switched from an eighty-hour a week trauma surgeon to Monday through Friday, plus every other Saturday morning general practitioner. It wasn't the extra free time that was an adjustment, although that was something to get used to. It was the patients. So far this morning I'd treated a man for chlamydia, handing him not only a prescription for antibiotics but some condom samples. After that, I pulled an eraser out of a six-year-old's ear and performed a newborn baby well-check.

"Doing okay?" Verna Jeffries asked, holding out a mug filled with steaming coffee over the check in counter as I walked by.

I slung my stethoscope around my neck and eagerly snagged it, mentally blessing her practical nature.

I scanned the waiting area–which was currently empty–as I took a sip. The practice was in a converted old house in the historic downtown area. The entry was the original family room, fireplace and all. The bedrooms had been converted into exam rooms. My office, which I shared with Dr. Jeffries–Verna's husband–was the old den.

This place was a long way from the hospital's clinical interior.

"Good coffee," I said, pleasantly surprised. The brew at the hospital in Denver was mostly a HAZMAT situation except for the ICU break room, which I frequented–*used to frequent*–way more than a surgeon based in the ER should.

"I get the beans from Steaming Hotties."

I knew the place because Mav wore its damned pink t-shirt often enough.

"To answer your question, yes. Doing okay. So far, so good," I replied, inwardly sighing. No one had died anyway, which was a distinct possibility of my old job.

But was treating sexually transmitted diseases the escape I really wanted?

I had enough money. I could quit entirely. Buy a boat that floated and sail the seven seas.

She laughed. Her dark eyes were filled with humor, although I expected it was at my expense. From what she told me this morning when she handed me the first batch of insurance paperwork, that she was a grandmother of three, liked to snowshoe and had the best sourdough starter in town.

I had no idea what the last meant, so I'd only nodded when she'd overshared. Or maybe she regular-shared and I was used to non-sharing. My previous co-workers didn't have lives outside of the hospital, like me, so we didn't have much to talk about besides tricky cases.

"It'll take some getting used to," I added diplomatically.

"Getting used to what?" she wondered. "Seeing this many patients in a day?"

On the computerized schedule I had twelve patients plus a one-hour window for call-in urgent visits like kids with unplanned ear infections.

I shook my head. "Having patients be conscious."

Because patients sedated and prepped for surgery didn't tell me their quirks and talents. If they did have chlamydia, it was the least of their worries.

With a head cock, she eyed me, as if giving me some kind of her own swift assessment, just like I gave to every patient when entering an exam room.

"I think you're going to find *all* your patients awake. Except for the babies. Those you might want asleep."

I considered the one I'd just seen, who'd been blissfully asleep except when he got an immunization and nodded. "Wise words."

Her head tipped the other way, down the hall. "Your eleven o'clock is in room one. Annual. London's probably done with vitals."

Verna held out her hand and I gave the coffee back, eyeing it wistfully.

"I'll take care of it," she said, as if I was dropping a child off at the first day of kindergarten instead of being separated from caffeine for thirty minutes.

London, the efficient and knowledgeable nurse, came out of the exam room. She handed me the open laptop. "She's ready for you. Since it's her annual, I have everything set out ready to go. Just stick your head out when you're ready to do the exam and I'll come back."

Annual. *Annual.*

Gynecologic annual. Not a cardiology annual or sports physical annual.

The newborn I saw earlier was... different for me. I hadn't held a baby in years. Couldn't remember the last time.

A woman's breasts and vagina I was well acquainted with, in a personal setting, not a professional one. Not since my OB/GYN rotation during residency and that had been for only a few weeks.

I was a doctor. I saw bodies all the time. This was clinical. Completely clinical. The woman wasn't imminently dying from a car accident or fall. Easy. Get in, get out. Literally.

I knocked on the door, opened it and entered, glancing at the name on the patient record on the laptop screen.

Mallory Mornay.

"Miss Mornay, I'm Dr. James and I understand you're here for your–"

My words dropped off when I finally lifted my gaze to the woman who sat on the exam table.

Mallory Mornay. I said the name aloud, but I didn't put it together until now.

Not Mallory Mornay, the random woman who was here for a woman's annual reproductive health screening.

This was Mallory. *Mallory.*

Bridget's best friend Mallory, who was outgoing, vivacious, and extroverted. Sexy and bold. Hot as hell and the woman I dreamed about fucking ever since I first met her in July. She was a goodie-goodie first grade teacher and I always wanted to dirty her up. Do filthy things to her. *With* her.

And she was sitting here in a paper gown, ready to part her legs nice and wide.

And not in the way I'd been imagining in the shower as I rubbed one out. Fuck. FUCK!

2

MALLORY

Oh my God.

Oh.

My.

God. No... gosh.

I shifted on the exam table and the paper beneath my bare butt crinkled. So did the ridiculous gown I was wearing.

Theo James just came in the door of my woman's appointment. With a beard on his rugged face that he hadn't had the last time I saw him. That was just unfair.

Theo James.

And he was the doctor. Who was going to look at my vagina. Literally sit on a stool between my spread legs with a light shining on it. He was going to put his fingers *in it.*

God, was my wax okay? I shaved my legs, but did I use enough lotion? I didn't want to have alligator scale calves.

Oh crap, I kept my rubber ducky socks on because it was pet week at school. If socks weren't bad enough, what about all my nooks and crannies? Were they normal? Was one side bigger than the other for all women? What about inside? How was it supposed to look? Was he going to peek and run away? Or worse, laugh?

I wanted to have a hot and sexy vagina. Pussy. Whatever Lindy wrote in her romance books. But when I looked at mine with a handheld mirror, it didn't look hot. Maybe mine was–

"Mallory?"

His deep voice had me blinking. Sh–sugar.

I gave him a wide smile. "Sorry. Um, what are you doing here?"

"Dr. Robinson retired. I've taken her place."

Dr. Robinson retired? Just like that?

"Here? I mean, now? I mean..." I closed my eyes because I felt like a moron. Of course Theo worked here. Now. He didn't wear a stethoscope around his neck–which was really flipping sexy–and walk into a woman's health exam willy-nilly.

Did he?

He came all the way into the room, set the laptop down on the counter across from me, then leaned against it.

I'd seen him in casual clothes before. The three times I'd seen him. Yes, I was counting. The first time was in the wallpaper photo on Mav's laptop. The second, at my brother Arlo's bar the week Bridget met Mav. And the third, the night I went to Mav's–and Bridget's–place for barbeque and he was just... there for an impromptu visit. Every time he'd been casual in jeans. Now? He had on a white doctor coat over a pair of khakis and a white dress shirt. He even had on a tie.

A tie! I squirmed on the table.

Crinkle!

Gah. Sit still, Mal!

The tie did it for me, but so did the doctor's coat. So did everything about him. One look at his photo back in July and I'd told Bridget I was going to marry him. Yes, I was crazy. Yes, I lusted after him. Why? I had no idea.

Every time we met, he was quiet and broody. Intense. Totally not my type. Except my ovaries popped out an egg every time I breathed in his dark man scent. Was it cologne or body wash? And my vagina, it got wet. Very wet. Like Slip and Slide on a hot summer day kind of wet.

Which meant...

Squirm. *Crinkle.*

I was wet now. Naked beneath a gown. And he was going to find out.

Did other women get wet for their doctor? Did he–or she–discover it when they did the exam? Wait, how many vaginas had he examined before... as a doctor? I was suddenly jealous and freaked. Maybe mine wasn't on the same vagina league as the others. I was short and curvy. Some gorgeous women, all willowy and tall, had to have an equally gorgeous vagina.

She had to.

What did I know? I'd never done this before!

"Mallory?"

I startled and met his dark gaze. "Yes. Hi, Theo. I mean, Dr. James."

The corner of his mouth tipped up. "Theo's fine, unless

you'd be more comfortable calling me Dr. James in this setting. You're here for a gynecological exam. I know this is a small town and everyone seems to know everyone else."

"Just like this, right?"

It was possible the corner of his mouth quirked a little more, but I couldn't be sure.

"Exactly. I'm sure I'll meet many people I will treat at the grocery store or a restaurant. But this is different. You're different."

You're different.

My heart leapt and I clasped my hands in my lap with secret glee. Except he didn't mean it as praise. He didn't mean it as *You're different from every woman I've ever met, and I haven't stopped thinking about you or wanting to fuck you so hard you forget your name.*

"You mean because I'm Bridget's friend and she's all hot and heavy with your brother. Then there's Lindy, who's more a mom to me than my own, with your *other* brother," I clarified, bringing myself back to reality.

He nodded. "I can reschedule you and have Dr. Jeffries do your exam if you'd feel more comfortable."

He was the other doctor in the practice, but I'd never seen him except one time when I was nine and had strep. He was nice, but he was old. Well, probably not old, but not young. And a man. A nice man, but a man. I always stuck with Dr. Robinson, a woman. Until now.

Theo was rejecting me. Did he not want to see my vagina? All of a sudden, I wasn't doubting my vagina, I was proud of it. Mine was as good as any other woman's! I was going to stand up for my lady parts. He was a doctor and I needed birth control. Just because I avoided all male doctors until now didn't prove I was hot for Theo. I admitted–and had told Bridget for months–that I lusted after him and wanted to marry him.

It didn't mean we couldn't behave in a patient/doctor manner. Right?

"If you don't treat women who are Bridget's friends, you're going to lose a lot of business," I advised.

He nodded. "Probably true. If you're comfortable with me... with the visit, then we will proceed. The nurse will be in the room during the exam, but first we can go over your health, any questions or concerns you have. Do you still want me?"

I swallowed. Gosh, this was hell.

Of course I still wanted him.

Between my thighs.

Fu–dge! If there ever was a *be careful what you wish for* situation, this was it.

3

THEO

I watched her squirm, then that pert little chin tipped up.

"It's fine."

"Good. This will be just like your last exam, so no surprises. Except me, I guess."

She bit her lip and glanced at the tray with the supplies. "I, um... I've never had one of these exams before."

I grabbed the laptop again, tucked it into my left forearm and scrolled through her records. "You're twenty—"

"Four."

I glanced at her date of birth–not that I doubted she knew her age–did some speed math. Her birthday was last month.

"You've been a patient of Dr. Robinson since..."

"All my life," she finished for me again.

I looked up from the screen. It seemed odd that Dr. Robinson never performed a pelvic exam on her before. Twenty-four was pretty old for not having one. I wasn't going to share that with Mallory though. I'd only talked to the doctor once on the phone and she seemed competent, which meant there was a reason.

"Okay." I nodded and scanned the report again, but it was impossible to go through a lifetime of records right now. "Your vitals are good. Last menstrual period was ten days ago."

I set the laptop back on the counter, dropped into the wheeled stool and leaned against the counter so there was as much space between us as possible. She had her ankles crossed and the paper gown tucked around her and below her knees. I'd seen her less covered over the summer. Then, I didn't remember her wearing ridiculous socks with ducks on them. "Are you having any problems you'd like to talk about?"

She recrossed her ankles.

"I want to go on birth control. Dr. Robinson said when I was ready, she'd put me on it."

My back went straight, and I narrowed my eyes. "Condoms are the safest option for contraception because it protects from sexually transmitted diseases that other methods don't. However, being on another form, a backup method, is very important for women in case of user error or breakage."

I couldn't believe Dr. Robinson didn't protect her female patients, or at least empower them, in their sexual health. And Mallory was smart.

"Is there a reason I didn't see in your records" –I

thumbed toward the laptop– "that prohibits you from being on it before now? Family history? Blood clots or cancer?"

She shook her head.

"You've been using condoms exclusively and consistently?"

She shook her head again.

I stood, set my hands on my hips. What the fuck? I knew she was a little wild. Fun, definitely. But reckless? "Mallory, you're risking–"

"I don't have sex."

I blinked.

She didn't have sex. She hadn't had a pelvic exam and wasn't on birth control, which meant–

"You're a virgin?" I asked, trying to keep my voice even. Professional.

And my dick down. Mallory Mornay wasn't just the leading star of my every fantasy, but also hadn't been touched. God, the thought of her on her knees, looking up at me seeing a dick for the first time–mine–and asking me what she needed to do to satisfy me had me instantly hard. I grabbed the laptop, slammed the lid down and held the thing in front of my crotch.

If Mallory saw how hard I was, she'd lose her shit, and rightfully so. I could lose my job or my license or–

"I'm not a virgin. I had sex once. I was sixteen. It's not in there." She looked pointedly at the laptop. No way in hell was I lifting it to read back through her history to see if she was telling the truth. She was. Why would she lie? And she was doing a shit job if she was. "I didn't tell Dr. Robinson because it didn't go real well."

She looked at her hands in her lap.

I dropped back in the chair... carefully and kept the laptop in front of me. "Did he hurt you?" My voice was low and deep usually, but now? It came out almost a growl.

I'd find him and kill him.

Her head whipped up, pale eyes wide.

She tucked her long blonde hair behind her ear, clearly flustered. "No, I mean, it hurt because first time and all, but he just... God, he stuck it in twice and then popped out and came in the condom. He wasn't even inside me for more than three seconds."

If the guy had also been sixteen, it was a realistic scenario for a first time. Zero control and Mallory's untried pussy? I was impressed he was a two-pump chump instead of only one. The fact that he came just kneeling between her thighs was something I was starting to understand.

And I wasn't a horny teenager either. Hell, I was a horny thirty-something, which made me... what? Desperate? Weak?

Doing some more math, that fateful event was eight years ago and all she got was in and out, in and out? It didn't sound like he got her off or any kind of pleasure.

That was worse than her being a virgin. A gorgeous woman like Mallory *not* having sex? It was a travesty. I had so many questions, but they weren't professional. Or medical.

"Then you wish to have birth control now because you are going to have sex." It was a deduction, but I knew I was accurate. She said she'd come in and see Dr. Robinson when she was ready. Which was now.

She nodded. "Yes. Like you said, I want to protect

myself. I do *not* want kids. There's a guy, a teacher at the high school with Bridget, and I'm going to have sex with him."

Like hell she was.

4

MALLORY

I MET Bridget on the sidewalk outside of the yoga studio. A chilly breeze blew down the street and I shivered. The snow from the storm the week before was gone, but fall had definitely set in. Her cheeks were all flushed and I wasn't sure if it was from the cold or if she just came from a different kind of exercise with Mav.

The bitch.

I loved her, but her happiness made me grumpy. She was getting some and I definitely was not.

The scent of garlic and marinara sauce made me hungry enough to skip our friend Aspen's class and hit up her brother's pizza shop instead, but I wasn't telling Bridget that. She didn't like yoga and I practically forced her to show up. I had news and I wanted to share.

Bridget was in yoga pants, a thick puffy coat and hat. Her worn running shoes were on her feet and she had a disgruntled look on her face. "You know I don't like yoga. And I ran five miles this morning."

See?

"Go–sh, how about some cheese with that whine?" I asked, grabbing her arm and pulling her toward the studio's door. I wasn't going to tell her I wasn't as motivated as I let on.

"Mmm, cheese," she said, practically moaning as she lifted her nose in the air like a bloodhound.

"Yeah, cheese. I love cheese, too."

"Then let's get pizza," she pleaded. "You can tell me whatever it is you're dying to share over pizza better than from downward dog."

She did have a good point. And it did smell so dang good.

"Is it Cheryl again?" she asked.

Cheryl was my mother. Bridget had known her forever and a half and knew all the drama. I called her by first name because while she'd birthed me–we looked too much alike for there to be doubt–I'd pretty much taken care of her instead of the other way around. To have a drunk and pretty much a deadbeat for a mother, well... both parents, and growing up happened fast.

Ironic that my brother owned a bar considering what we went through.

"This week?" I clarified, then shook my head. I pushed off the sour feeling whenever Cheryl came up. "No. I covered their rent, so she's been quiet. As far as I know she's still cleaning rooms up at the resort so she hasn't asked me to pay the electric bill. *Yet.*"

Bridge nodded in commiseration. My mother went

through jobs like most people went through groceries. Getting new ones every week or so and moaning about how she struggled and suffered. As for my father? He was a oil service technician at a local lube and tire shop. He gave the bare minimum in effort and got minimum wage for it. Then again, the owners weren't expecting much from him so he never made manager even after twenty years. I had a feeling they kept him employed because they knew he wouldn't get hired anywhere else and had a soft spot for me and Arlo, even now that we were adults.

Dad was harmless. His goal in life was to sit in his worn recliner watching TV while working his way through a case of beer without falling asleep with a lit cigarette in his hand. And it also meant he was useless. Pretty crappy of me to say about my own father, but facts were facts. This meant that I spent tons of time at Bridge's house growing up and the only people at my high school and college graduations clapping for me were Arlo, Bridge, and Lindy.

The only trips my parents went on–because they had zero money–were guilt trips and took me along for the ride. That was why I was still living with a roommate instead of my own place. A chunk of my salary went to my parents which made it really hard to save for a down payment on a place of my own. I had a steady paycheck with benefits and all that, but a teacher's income wasn't huge.

"You need to cut her off," she advised, just like she had for a long time. "How come she doesn't pester your brother?"

"Because she always made it clear that he wasn't hers." She was his stepmother. "Because of that, she knows he won't give her any money." Arlo had cut the cord with them a while ago.

"Then it clearly works."

I sighed. "I know. I know. I don't want to talk about her. I went to the doctor today," I said. I threw it right on out there.

She frowned, then gripped my hand. "Is there something wrong?"

"What? No. I mean, well, I don't know. It was just an annual exam."

"You don't know? Like you need tests done? They found a lump?" Her eyes got bigger at the same time her voice went up a notch.

I scowled, thinking about a lump. "Jeez, Bridge, no."

"Can you please say Jesus and God and fuck and shit like everyone else? I can't have you talking about a tumor and saying golly gee."

I crossed my arms over my coat. "I dropped the f-bomb the other day in class. You know six-year-olds all go home and tell their parents. No one's come in to complain, thankfully. That happened twice last year as well and–"

"Fine. No swearing. Tell me about the gosh darn tumor."

I opened the door and stepped into the warm entry, hit immediately by the scent of lavender and soft yoga music. It had lutes or flutes and had rain sounds, which always made me have to pee.

There was space for a bench and cubbies for shoes, then a stairwell to the second floor. The yoga studio was above the pizza place. "There is no tumor. God. Fuck. Dammit, woman, you're crazy."

She dropped onto the bench. "Then why don't you know if something's wrong?"

I took a deep breath and set my yoga bag–with my rolled-up mat sticking out the top–on the floor. "I didn't go in because something was wrong. I went in for birth control. And I didn't get examined because Theo was the doctor, and he doesn't like my vagina."

Bridget blinked at me once, then popped to her feet. She snagged my bag with one hand, my wrist with the other and pulled me back out onto the street.

I chased after her—I had no choice really since she had a death grip on me–as she pulled me into the pizza place and to a corner table. She practically pushed me into a chair, then turned. "Otis, two glasses of Chianti. No, make it a bottle."

Then she dropped into the seat across from me and pushed her glasses up her nose. "Start talking. Theo, as in Theo James, Mav's brother, right?"

I nodded.

"Theo saw your vagina and told you he doesn't like it?"

Otis appeared with a bottle and two glasses. Maybe because he had a sister or because he was smart, he eyed us, then backed away carefully. Maybe he heard what Bridge just asked me and I wouldn't blame him for his cautious retreat. It was a loaded question.

I poured and Bridge shrugged out of her jacket. The place was warm from the huge pizza ovens and so much better than yoga.

"He never saw it," I explained. "I was in a paper gown, and he came in. That was a shock, I'll tell you."

"He arrived last week during the snowstorm and told us he was moving here and taking a job at a family practice."

I took a sip–no, swig–of the wine, then asked, "You knew since last week? Why didn't you tell me?"

"I know, you keep saying you're going to marry him."

I looked down at my glass. "Well, maybe not since he rejected me."

"He rejected you?" She leaned in and lowered her voice. "What did you do, put your feet in the stirrups and say fuck me?"

My eyes widened at that visual. "Gosh, Bridge, do you think that's my style?"

I really hoped not. But... it was kinda hot if we were playing sexy games. If we skipped the speculum and all that.

She rolled her eyes. "Spill."

I pushed her full glass in front of her. "Drink and shut up."

She frowned but did as I ordered.

"He told me Dr. Robinson retired and he took her place."

She saw Dr. Robinson growing up too. Half the town probably had.

"We talked some about my medical history and I told him I was in for an annual exam because I wanted birth control."

"Got all that."

I reached across the table and pushed the glass closer to her mouth.

"I told him I was going to start having sex and that I

wanted to protect myself. Then he referred me to a gynecologist."

He'd changed his mind about Dr. Jeffries and put in a referral for me instead.

"That's it?"

I nodded and took another gulp. "He didn't want to see my vagina."

She frowned. "This wasn't a date. He was doing his job, which now is a family doctor. If you're going on birth control and need an annual exam, then it makes sense for him to refer you. His background is in trauma surgery. I'm sure he's no expert on inserting IUDs."

"I have no doubt he's good at inserting *something* into a vagina."

She laughed and gave me an appalled look.

"I'm sure I'm right," I continued. "Besides, he knew what he was walking into when he took the job because it's a flipping family practice. If he's waiting for someone to walk in with a trauma emergency, he's dumber than I thought."

"I haven't been to Dr. Robinson in years," she commented.

"You went to Boston. It's kinda hard to see her when you're in a different time zone."

"She would have referred you on to an OBGYN, too."

I knew it, but wow, Theo James.

"So he wasn't rejecting me." I was being weird. I knew it. But I was always this way. I didn't like shame. Not that he'd shamed me, but I felt rejected, just like I said. It was a trigger for me because I was used to it. Cheryl wasn't a hugger, or even a liker. She was a moocher.

"Not you or your vagina," she added. "Besides, if you're so gung-ho about marrying him, why are you going on that date with the history teacher?"

She knew all about the date because she was the one to fix us up in the first place. She'd been working as a long-term sub teaching physics just down the hall from him since August. He was cute, nice and well... fuckable. Except–

"I didn't even know Theo moved into town until I was sitting in a paper gown. Also, because I have no clue what I'm doing," I reminded. "You think a guy like Theo wants a clueless woman in his bed? I need experience. Skills. Talent. Besides Mr. History Guy, I'm going to Las Vegas for that bachelorette party. You remember I told you about it."

"Right, your friend Alana from college."

While Bridge went to MIT on a full ride, I went to a state school. I'd had a few small scholarships that cut down the tuition, plus I did work study to cover some more. Even after eating ramen and taking classes over the summer to be done in three years instead of four, I still had student loans. I barely had enough to scrape up money for a ticket to Vegas.

I nodded. "Vegas is *the* place to do crazy things. I mean, Lindy and Dex got *married* at a drive thru chapel and don't remember it."

"There's a big difference between what they did and you hooking up with a stranger in Sin City."

"I know, but I want to be prepared. If I'm going to have sex with Mr. History Guy—"

"His name is Tom. You make him sound like he's

seventy and teaches kids cool historical facts on a community TV program."

I rolled my eyes. "Fine. Tom. If I'm going to do it with him, why can't I do it with a guy in Vegas?"

She reached out, gave my hand a squeeze. "You can. You'll have guys in Vegas eating out of your hand."

"I have other places on my body I'd rather them eating out."

She closed her eyes and shook her head slowly. "Well, don't get arrested, whatever you do."

I sputtered, which had her looking at me again. "I can't believe you think I'd get arrested."

It was her turn to roll her eyes.

"What? I'm not that wild and crazy." I leaned in. "I've been saving it up for Tom, a high school history teacher. How exciting is that?"

She wagged her head from side to side as if considering my words more than required. "You've been saving it up for Theo since you first saw his picture. But Tom's okay. He's actually pretty hot. Not James brothers hot, but he'll do."

That made me frown. "Yeah, a James brother doesn't even want to see my untalented vagina."

She pushed her glasses up, then narrowed her eyes. With a swivel in her seat, she called, "Otis!"

I watched as he held his hands up for the pizza dough he tossed in the air, catching it deftly so it wilted down past his wrists, then flung it again. "Yeah?"

"A large with olives and triple cheese."

"On it," he called.

A few other tables were occupied, but there was

nothing new about the casual environment. Bridget shouting her order was normal.

Bridge looked to me, her eyes large behind her glasses. "You are always so hard on yourself."

"Me? *I'm* hard on myself?" I countered.

"We're talking about you. Guys are not looking for talented vaginas. You're making them out to be way smarter than they really are."

"Vaginas?"

"Men."

Otis brought over plates, silverware, and napkins.

"Otis, you're a guy," I said.

He was older than us. Cute. I'd date him if he didn't seem like a brother since he was good friends with *my* brother, Arlo.

"I'm glad you noticed." He inhaled, puffing up his chest beneath the pizza place t-shirt.

"And single," I added.

He took a step back and held his palms out, glancing between us. "Whoa, Bridge is taken. Very taken. Have you seen her man? He's a fucking lumberjack. And you're... well, you're you. No way are we dating."

I frowned. "If I didn't think of you as a weird brother, I'd be insulted."

He huffed and dropped his hands. "What's the question? I know you've got one."

"Are you looking for talent in a vagina?"

His dark eyebrows rose so far, they were hidden by his unruly hair. "What the hell does that mean?"

"If you started dating a woman and found out she didn't

have lots of experience in bed, would that be an issue for you?"

"Is she legal?"

We both frowned and said, "YES!"

"Then no. I'm not looking for a *talented* vagina. It's fun to see what a woman finds hot. What makes her get all–"

Now it was my turn to hold up my hand to stop him. "Okay, we get the idea. Stop there before I get too nauseated imagining you having sex to eat our pizza that better be in the oven."

His hand went to his chest. "I'm not that bad."

"Do you want us to talk about Aspen's sex life?"

He shivered, just like any brother would. "Fuck no."

"Fine. So no talent needed. Thanks."

He nodded, then once again backed away slowly and carefully.

"See?" Bridge asked, which was totally annoying.

"I'm getting birth control and getting laid."

"I get all that, but why now? Why all of a sudden? You've been all hot and bothered for Theo for months."

I wasn't going to tell her there'd been a wet spot on the back of my paper gown when I got up to get redressed earlier. I was hot for Theo James. H.O.T.

That was when I thought he didn't live in town. Now? I could run into him anywhere, anytime.

"Me and my vagina aren't sitting around waiting for a guy like him to notice me. I was naked, Bridge, and he turned me down."

"Okay, what you're suggesting is a little creepy if I think about it a little too long."

"What you're saying is if you think about it a little less, it's kinda hot."

She looked away because she was right there with me. "Fine, but he didn't turn you down. He was *working*."

I shrugged. "I'm horny, Bridge. I want sex. I've earned it."

"I agree. So have it with Theo. *Not* on an exam table. You know, the guy you're going to marry."

I shrugged and waved my hand through the air to try to downplay the fact that she mentioned that three times. Maybe I'd overdone it in the past few months. He was gorgeous and up close, in person, gah. I melted. My brain turned to mush or baked beans or something.

"It's just talk and no one woman wants to have an ugly vagina. Obviously. You know me, gab, gab, gab."

Yes, I wanted him, and I lusted after him. Did I ever really think he'd want me? No. But Bridge knew I was a big blabbermouth and usually just smiled and nodded like I did with my first graders when one told me she wanted to be an ant so she could carry things over ten times their body weight.

Sure, it was one thing to want Theo and feel hurt when he referred me to a gynecologist, as weird as all that sounded; if I didn't have those baked beans for brains, I'd see that it was the proper response.

It was another thing to actually marry the guy. I learned from my parents not to expect much. I'd been emotionally hurt by them often enough to know better. That a guy like Theo wouldn't love me. It was easier just to be casual, to talk a big game and sleep with Tom the History Teacher.

Dr. Theo James was in a completely different league. He

had it all. Brains, brawn, beauty, and billions. And most likely a big dick.

She studied me. "You sure, because I saw him with his beard and he's really hot. Don't tell Mav."

I rolled my eyes. Like Maverick James would feel threatened by any man, even his brother.

I played it off even more. "Seriously, I want to take something for a ride besides my vibrator and Tom's not a bad option."

The history teacher would do.

"I'm not looking for roses and candlelight, Bridge. I'm also tired of waiting. It's happening. I want up against the wall kind of sex. Maybe bent over a couch or something. I'm twenty-four. It's time."

"But Theo–"

I cut her off. "You can't set me up with Tom and then be Team Theo. It's just sex, Bridge. So shut up and go get our pizza."

5

THEO

"After Dr. Footsie, I'm surprised you're not a born-again virgin."

Mav and I were on the couch in Dex's little rental house. Or my rental now. Dex's contract on the place expired when he returned to the Silvermines at the start of the hockey season. Since he and Lindy were hot and heavy, they had her house to stay in when they came back to town.

Silas–the other brother–and I agreed we'd keep this renovated miner's shack for ourselves since it seemed we popped into Hunter Valley often enough and we didn't want to stay with Mav and Bridge like the first few visits. The very first time we checked on him back in July, Bridget had bolted from the place in only a sheet.

Yeah, a different house was required.

When I accepted the job at the medical practice, I already had a place to stay.

"Maude? Why are you bringing her up now?" I asked, tipping back my beer.

Mav brought a six-pack and we'd settled in to watch one of Dex's games on TV. It was in Buffalo, and he'd already scored two goals. Between finding his woman and being one of the season's top scorers, he was one happy fucker.

"Wondering if she's the reason you bailed on being a trauma surgeon and took a job in a small Montana town."

I had no doubt he, Bridget, Dex, Lindy, Silas... hell, even the head of surgical operations, wanted to know the real reason I bailed on that kind of career track.

I sighed, slumped lower on the couch. Scout, Mav's dog, was between us, belly up, short little legs toward the ceiling, snoring. He didn't stir. He had zero shame, and I was a little jealous.

"You think I let a woman dictate my life?" I pushed. I hadn't thought about Maude since the day I walked into the third-floor doctor's lounge and found her and one of the colorectal guys getting it on. And by getting it on, I meant they were on the bench in the locker area, and she was using her bare feet to work his dick.

I'd had no interest in seeing the dude's dick and I definitely didn't need to know Maude had some kinks she hadn't pulled out when we fucked. Of course, we fucked in the same locker room, but I had her pressed against a locker and my dick was surrounded by her pussy, not her feet.

It meant I hadn't been all that interested in finding out Maude's needs, and she hadn't been interested enough in me to share hers.

So when I turned on my heel and left them to their fun,

I hadn't looked back. Literally and figuratively.

For some fucked up reason, I had a different woman who filled my head these days. Mallory, the complete opposite of her best friend, Bridget. Mallory was outgoing, vivacious, a loudmouth and... hot. Now I knew things about her that only made her hotter. And I couldn't tell my brother or anyone else because of patient privacy laws. Not that I would ever announce that Mallory was pretty much a virgin or that she was on the prowl. While I might not act like one when fucking, I was a gentleman. I wasn't going to sit around and tell Mav such private things about Mallory. We weren't women with wine. We were men with beers and hockey. But knowing her secrets... I was going to be the gentleman who fucked Mallory instead of some rando high school teacher.

She said she wanted to have sex. That it was time. *Time.* As if it was something to check off one of Lindy's infamous to-do lists. Although if it was on Lindy's list, no doubt Dex would happily check that off for her. Mallory didn't seem to want rainbows and fucking unicorns. Harps and candlelight. It seemed sex to her didn't have to mean a relationship.

I could totally relate. Who wanted a relationship? All they were was fucked up. Being raised by a narcissist would do that to a guy. Except Mav and Dex were proving finding the right woman didn't mean a fucked-up love.

They fell for their women. Fell hard, and fast.

As for me? With Mallory, it would be a community service to her, offering her my dick and other skills where her clit was concerned. And her nipples. Shit, and her pussy, which had to be so fucking tight.

I shifted on the couch because my dick was fucking hard at the wrong time. Again. Second time in one day.

I'd never gotten hard for a patient before. Never. Then one twenty-four-year-old teacher in a paper gown and duck socks and the damned thing wouldn't go down.

Mav turned his gaze from the TV and eyed me.

"Maude's long gone," I promised. "Thank fuck. But you? You're so whipped you're sitting here for the hour your woman's at yoga."

He shrugged his broad shoulders, completely unaffected by me taking a swipe at his man card. "Maybe, but she's going to be all nice and flexible when she's done taking the class with Mal. She does the bending and stretching, and I get all the perks."

Mav grinned. Actually grinned.

I frowned. The fucker just had to drop that Mallory was doing yoga as well. Instantly, an image of her in tight leggings, bent over with her ass in the air, filled my head. Maybe I'd take her that way first and show her how good it could be from behind. I'd pull her hair and she'd–

Fuck. Fuck! Stop thinking about it. Her. If Mav saw how I was getting hard, there would be problems. I didn't have a laptop to hide behind.

So I switched back to Maude, which was a perfect dick deflator. "You know I didn't move here because of Maude."

"Then why? It's like that hospital was your man cave."

I'd shown up the week before in an early snowstorm, unannounced and dropped the bomb on him and Bridget that I was moving here. Six months ago, I wouldn't have believed it either.

"All I saw in Denver was the inside of the hospital or

inside of a body. For years. I'm unfeeling."

"Cleary, since you fucked Maude."

I frowned but didn't argue with him. She was definitely a sign of my numbness.

"A kid came in. MVA. Stupid parents didn't put his seatbelt on him and got in an accident. Ejected. Lost an arm from that, barely alive in the ER. Ended up dying on the operating table."

"Shit, dude. I'm sorry."

I shook my head, remembering looking at the clock on the wall in the OR and calling the time of death.

"I didn't feel anything. I think back, still don't. I should. Fuck, I'm totally broken. A child died horribly when it was completely preventable. I could've been at the grocery store picking out toilet paper for all the emotion I felt over it."

Mav stayed quiet, just took a pull of beer. The hockey announcer's voice followed the game on screen, but I wasn't paying it any attention.

"Last week I was at a conference in Arizona and Bradley called me and told me about this job opening and I–"

"Yeah, what the fuck's that about?" Mav cut in to ask. "He was head hunting for you?"

I sat up, placed my beer on the chunk of wood that served as a coffee table, rested my elbows on my knees. "No. I never asked him to do anything like that. He's your assistant. But he's a horse whisperer or something."

"That make you the horse?"

I shrugged. "He called me and said there was an opening at a practice here and I should consider it. Said it was Monday through Friday and every other Saturday morning. No surgery. No one dies."

"Hell, I'd take that job," he replied. Before he met Bridget and pretty much relocated to Hunter Valley, he worked sixty to eighty hour weeks. Now he focused solely on the James Inn sector he was building, but the one here in Hunter Valley specifically. "What makes you think you'll start caring for patients here?"

I shrugged, thinking of the mix of locals I saw today. STD, vaccinations, ear infections, strep throat, and... Mallory.

I sure as shit felt something when I was with Mallory. Lust. Desire. Attraction. Need. Jealousy. Possessiveness.

Probably not the correct emotions and feelings, but what the hell did I know? I was fucked up when it came to relating and empathizing with others.

"I was standing there in the middle of the conference and I said fuck it," I continued. "Fuck it all."

I couldn't believe I did it, but here I was. Drinking beer with my brother instead of pulling another twenty-four-hour shift at the hospital. That was exactly where I'd be at this moment.

"You're going to miss surgery though," he said, mansplaining my job to me. "The ER. The rush. I mean, it's what you do."

I shrugged because what did he know about being a doctor or dealing with dying patients day in and day out? But he wasn't talking about them. He was talking about me.

"Maybe I'll see if they're looking for a part-timer at the hospital here. A sub like Bridge at the high school. But for now? Today? I get to sit on my ass drinking beer with my brother while my other one is on TV scoring goals."

Mav looked at his watch and stood. Scout stirred,

flipped over, and hopped to the floor to stand beside his human. "Speaking of scoring. Gotta pick up Bridge."

"Fucker," I said with a grin. I was happy for him. I'd never imagined a twenty-two-year-old would be what he needed, but my life was a cluster fuck. Who was I to question?

"Get a woman of your own," he snapped, but without any heat since he was grinning. "One who isn't part reptile or have a foot fetish."

Instantly, I thought of Mallory. She definitely ran hot, and I doubted she had a thing for feet. I wondered then what she had a thing for. Being sassy and getting punished for it. Definitely. Maybe a little exhibitionism. Or–

Hell, she was pretty much a virgin. She probably didn't know what got her hot. Fuck, wouldn't that be fun to find out. To make her squirm and squi–

"Earth to Theo," Mav said, waving his hand in front of my face.

I blinked.

"Are you having a stroke?"

I frowned. "What? Fuck, no."

"Then where the fuck did you just go?"

I frowned even deeper. "You don't want to know."

He studied me. "Yeah, I probably don't."

I stood and he smacked me on the shoulder. "Glad you're in town. Oh, Bridge says to tell you dinner tomorrow night. I know you'll be there because one, you can't cook. Two, you just told me you have a normal person's schedule. Three, you have no life."

"You had me at *I can't cook*."

6

MALLORY

WHICH SAID *FUCK ME* BETTER? The yellow lace or the red satin? Both were newly purchased off the clearance rack just for tonight. And Vegas. Wearing my ratty flannel robe, I stared at the options I put out on my bed before my shower. I thought of Tom. From the photos I saw, he was handsome. Bridge's classroom was across the hall from his and she said he was nice. Got along well with his students. A little goofy.

Bridge hadn't said he was hot. Or sexy. Or had big dick energy. Or... well, she wouldn't. Compared to Mav, Tom probably looked like a garden gnome to her.

"Done in the bathroom?" Maggie called through my closed bedroom door.

"Yes!"

My roommate and I had gone to high school together but hadn't ever hung out. But after college, I'd heard she was looking for a roommate to sublet because her old one had moved out. I was desperate not to move in with my parents and jumped at the opening. We were friendly, but not tight, which worked out fine.

As an agricultural rep, she traveled a fair amount. Plus, she had a boyfriend who lived in Havre, a few hours away. She stayed with him as much as she was here. She'd been hinting at moving in with him because they'd gotten pretty serious, which meant I'd have to float the entire rent on my own. A teacher's salary wasn't huge, and while it was consistent and had good benefits, renting solo would cost more than owning. At least for the little house I had my eye on. Mrs. Jonsdottir, who'd been a teacher at the elementary school for over forty years, had the cutest little place and I wanted it.

Bad.

Crazy bad. Hopefully Maggie could relocate to Havre at the same time I bought my dream house.

Mrs. Jonsdottir mentioned time and again that she wanted to sell and move closer to her children who'd long ago moved out of state. Every time I saw her, I reminded her I wanted to buy it from her, and she always said she'd talk to me first before she did anything. But she'd yet to sell.

In the meantime, I was saving hard for it and was careful with my expenses. Fortunately, for the Vegas bachelorette trip, I'd only needed to pay airfare and food. Hotel was covered.

I looked around my room. Even though I'd lived here for over a year, it felt... temporary. *I* felt that way. Like I didn't know where I belonged. I needed something of my own. A place where I could paint the walls and walk around in my underwear. That I could do with what I wanted. Or fuck who I wanted. When I wanted it. And where. It wasn't like I could get a guy to fuck me on Maggie's mom's hand-me-down kitchen table or over the back of the couch she'd picked up at the thrift store.

"I'm too old for this," I muttered to myself.

I snagged the yellow lace panties, slipped them on. They didn't say seductress. I was *not* one of those. I had no clue what I was doing outside of watching porn and pretending my vibrator was an actual dick.

Go-sh, I was so nervous! Dinner with Tom was one thing, but being with him alone? Naked? He would see me. Only me. I couldn't hide behind my clothes or my sass or sarcasm. I wanted him to make me forget my own name.

"This is what happens, woman," I said aloud to myself. I wasn't getting a pep talk from my brother on this one. He knew about the date, but we didn't talk about our sex lives. I made that easy by not having one. "Get your shit together. Get naked. Get some dick-made orgasms."

After the pizza and pep talk the night before with Bridge, I'd coordinated via text with Tom for a date. Tonight. It was a school night, so neither of us were going to do anything wild and crazy. Well, I'd take wild and crazy as long as I was in bed by midnight.

By in bed, I meant asleep.

My cell rang and I grabbed it from the bedside table.

CHERYL.

"Fudge. Sugar. Dang. Carp. GAH!" I practically shouted. I hated to watch my cuss words, but if there was a time to swear, it was now.

She only called when she needed something, like money.

I glanced at the ceiling, then swiped the screen to answer her call. If I didn't talk to her now, she wouldn't stop. I wasn't going to let her mess with my date.

"Hey, Cheryl," I said, dropping onto my unmade bed.

"How's my pumpkin?"

I rolled my eyes.

"What's up?" I asked.

"Does something have to be up? Can't I want to talk to my only daughter?"

And it started.

"Yes," I said. "How're things? Dad?"

I could see her shrugging through the phone. "Fine. The shop was closed for two days. A water main burst down the street."

"I heard about that."

Small-town life meant nothing was a secret. When a tree fell on Bridge's and Lindy's house over the summer, news had spread within a few hours, and they'd had the entire town drive by to see it. I had to admit, it was a spectacle.

"Maybe you can stop by and visit with him since he's been a little bored without anything to do while he was off."

All he probably did was sit in his recliner, smoke, and watch TV, perfectly content.

"Sure."

"Bring some beers with you. Oh, and a quart of milk. Eggs. OJ. Bread."

She was out of money. Again.

"What happened to the extra cash I gave you at the beginning of the month with the rent?" I asked.

She sniffed. "There was a problem with the car and–"

"Dad fixes it at work."

"Like I said, a water main broke."

"So he couldn't fix it because of the water main?"

"He was busy."

"I thought you said he was bored."

I couldn't miss the huff through the phone.

"What's with all the questions?"

"Because I paid your rent this month and gave you a little over. You should have enough for extras... and I don't mean beer or your gin."

"What are you saying, that I'm not working hard enough?"

So much for being her little *pumpkin*.

"My salary only goes so far. I'm paying my bills and yours."

"All Miss High and Mighty now with that big job."

"I'm a first-grade teacher, not a hedge fund manager. The resort offers you overtime, I'm sure." If I had to pick up tutoring over the summer, she could add on some hours. "That's time-and-a-half?"

"Overtime?" She spat out the word as if it was foul tasting. "Your father needs me home to feed him his dinner."

"You mean open his beer," I muttered to myself.

"What?"

"Nothing."

"Why are you being so difficult?" I heard the familiar flick of a lighter, then a deep inhalation. The amount the two of them spent on cigarettes a month could cover their food bill. "After all the things we used our money on for you growing up, I'd think you'd be a little more grateful. Do you have any idea what I could have become if it wasn't for you?"

There was the knife she always liked to poke me with, laced with the poison of guilt and passive aggressiveness. The same old story she told about how I was an accident. That I'd never been wanted and that I, personally and solely, ruined my mother's life.

"Yes, I'm well aware you were to become the next top model or whatever it was, but you got pregnant with me and had to back out."

"You took my beauty, the least you can do is–"

I'd heard enough of this week's round of Mallory bashing. I was used to it, but it still sucked. "Just text me a list of groceries and I'll see if I can drop them by tomorrow. I have to go."

I hung up without saying goodbye, then tossed my phone aside, snagged the pretty yellow bra. My mother wasn't going to change. Not unless there was a time machine and she swallowed.

"Shit!" I shouted at the ceiling, not caring about swearing. Let it go, Mal. *Let it go.*

Yes, let it go, because I had a history teacher to fuck.

7

THEO

"I'M HERE!" I called from the front door. "You two better be dressed."

Scout scampered down the hallway to greet me just as Bridget stuck her head around the corner from the kitchen. She pushed her glasses up.

"Just missed the money shot of your brother's big dick," she said.

I held up my hand and winced. "You're one mean woman."

A grin spread across her face. "Just kidding. He's still at the site. They're installing all of the toilets today. Literally every single one. I had no idea one man could be so excited about them."

Leaning down, I gave Scout a pet and then joined Bridget in the kitchen.

"That's a lot of containers," I said, pointing to the center island.

"Well, it's *whatever-is-in-the-fridge* night. We're leaving tomorrow for Boston and don't want it to go to waste."

There were a pile of to-go boxes and plastic leftover tubs spread across the counter. She opened one and peeked inside.

"They finally got the professor?" I asked.

She glanced my way, a triumphant gleam in her eye. "We had him back in September, but two other women came forward with identical stories. The asshole. We decided to join forces so all three of us can get justice."

Just last year, Bridget had been a student at MIT and had her work stolen by one of her professors. He'd taken her thesis papers and published the findings as his, which had Bridget quickly kicked out for plagiarism. It had been her word against his. A coed versus a tenured professor at one of the most prestigious universities in the world. The situation was all kinds of fucked up, especially because she was the nicest–and smartest–woman I knew. She deserved her degree–which she hadn't been able to finish–and the accolades that went with her data. I knew nothing about math other than what was needed for dosing patients, but she sure as hell did.

"Justice? How about revenge?"

She shrugged and a slow smile spread across her young face. I still couldn't believe Mav had fallen for a twenty-two-year-old, but really, they were perfect for each other. He'd been clearly waiting for her, or some other romantic shit like that. When he found out what the asshole fucker had done... he'd gone ballistic. At least not in front of Bridget.

He put Bradley, the assistant extraordinaire and a team of private investigators to bring the guy down. After a few months, it looked like it was about to happen.

"I want to see him kicked out and to get my work back. If Mav wants to... well, whatever dark, alpha male thoughts he's hatched, that's up to him."

I had no doubt Mav had plans for the fucker. While I didn't think Mav would have him killed, because that would be too easy and quick, the guy would probably wish he was when Mav was done. He probably wouldn't be able to get a job teaching seals to play trumpets at the circus.

"I'm happy to help if needed," I added, but made a mental note to let Mav know that as well. "I know what to do with dead bodies."

A laugh ripped from her lips. "I'm sure you do. Mallory's just as ruthless."

I perked up at the name but didn't let it show. Ever since she left the doctor's office the day before, I'd been... unsettled. The idea of her having sex made me want to go all Mav and lumberjack the shit out of men in Hunter Valley who sniffed around her, let alone got his dick near her. It also made me a little crazy. Possessive, and I was *never* possessive. I could show Mallory what it was like with a real man, not some sixteen-year-old with pre-ejaculation issues.

She hadn't even come and that just pissed me off.

"From what I know of her, I have no doubt." I leaned against the counter and took the lid off a container. Pasta in a cream sauce with veggies. "She joining us? There's enough leftovers for ten people." I scanned the options, which was like a buffet.

"Ten? Or just you and Mav," she replied. She knew the James boys well. We were big eaters. "No, she's got a hot date." Bridget looked my way and waggled her eyebrows. "Dinner at The Lodge. I sorta fixed her up with the tenth-grade history teacher."

What the fuck? Mallory moved fast. I just saw her at her appointment. I grabbed another container, opened it with a little more aggression than necessary.

"On a Wednesday? An odd night for a date."

"A first date, not that it matters. If she hits it off with Tom on a Wednesday, then–"

I dropped the leftovers and looked at Bridget. "Tom? His name's Tom?"

Tom was a basic name. Plain. Boring. But common. Common was good because my first appointment the day before was a Tom whose dick itched, and it burned like fire when he pissed.

"Yeah."

I had a sinking feeling. This wasn't Denver where there were probably a hundred Toms in a one-mile radius. This was Hunter Valley, a small town in Montana. How many fucking Toms could there be?

I had to get answers from Bridget, but I couldn't tell her why. I couldn't tell her shit because of privacy laws. It was one thing to not want Mallory to fuck a history teacher, it was another to prevent her from fucking one with a sexually transmitted disease.

"I know a Tom," I murmured.

"Here in town? His last name's Zajik, which is different and memorable, but you've only been here a few days and you probably mean in Colo–"

Shit.

I didn't let Bridget finish because I got everything I needed. I bolted to the front door. "I have to go."

"What? Now? What's the matter?" she called, chasing after me. Scout came racing up and gave me a woof.

"Diarrhea."

"Wh–what?"

Yeah, I shocked the hell out of her. No one questioned diarrhea.

"Oh, um... well, this house has five bathrooms," she reminded as I kept moving. "You can have any one of them and I'll, um, leave you to it."

"No, not here," I called from the end of the walk.

"Um, okay, well, feel better!"

Like I said, no one bothered you when you had the shits. I was in my car and peeling down the driveway before Bridget had the front door closed.

Tom Zajik was Mr. STD. His raging case of chlamydia wasn't going to be resolved by the antibiotics I prescribed the day before. Which meant his dick was dangerous if he put it anywhere near Mallory's pussy... or her mouth.

Fuck me.

No, Tom was in danger if he got near Mallory. I wasn't sure what Mav had planned for that asshole MIT professor, but I was going to make it look like a little booboo in comparison if Mr. STD shared more than small talk with Mallory.

Fuck. Mallory was going to sleep with the guy. She made her intent clear. Her vagina was practically untried, and she wasn't protected by any birth control method besides condoms, even if she got in to see the OBGYN referral already.

She was any man's wet dream.

Hell, she was mine.

I had to stop her. To keep from fucking the wrong guy. Because if she wanted a dick, she'd get mine. Big, disease free, and all hers.

8

MALLORY

Tom Zajik was a nice guy. A ginger who looked like the actor from *Grey's Anatomy*, minus the Scottish accent, although he did seem to know quite about the history of Scotland, and the US Civil War. It wasn't all that exciting because I wasn't much of a history buff, but it did prove he was smart. A deep thinker. We spent dinner swapping student stories and the differences between teaching littles and teenagers. He was thoughtful, insightful, interesting, kinda cute, although only *handsome* like Bridge said. And he had the bladder of a peanut.

He paid the check, and we were leaving the restaurant when he diverted to the men's room near the entrance. He knew exactly where it was because he'd already gone twice. Yeah, peanut bladder.

I stood in the lobby waiting for him and stared up at the vaulted entry, the logs that made the entire place blend in with the whole western theme. Was this it? Would he ask me to go back to his place? Should I ask him to follow me home for a nightcap? Who said nightcap anyway? What *was* a nightcap?

Fudge. I thought I was supposed to be hot and bothered from being with a guy, not anxious and–

"Mal."

I spun on my cute heel I got at an end of season sale last year. My anxious thinking made me miss Tom's return.

And Theo.

Theo James.

What the... what? Why was Theo here?

They stood side by side eyeing me. Next to Theo, Tom was a golden retriever, all earnest and gentle, filled with random facts about something that happened a century ago. Theo was big, broad, and looked like a grumpy badass. Not that he appeared ready to kick the shit out of anyone, but his usual intense stare was in full force. I felt small, feminine, and a little flustered whenever I was in his vicinity. And my vagina? The one that was the topic of our conversation the day before? Yeah, her. She was into Theo, pretty much crying at the sight of him.

Which meant I got wet just looking at the guy.

Not Tom, my date, but Theo. The guy who appeared out of nowhere.

I looked from one, to the other, then back. My cheeks flushed and my heart rate kicked up so fast I got a head rush just like all the other times I ran into Theo.

"Theo..."

"You know him?" Tom asked, eyeing him and not in a good way. Like he had to pee again and wanted to do it on my leg. Maybe Tom was a little more manly than I thought.

I nodded, licked my lower lip. "This is Bridget's boyfriend's brother." Since Tom knew Bridget from work, he didn't need further explanation.

I looked to Theo. "What... what are you doing here?"

Tom and Theo shifted to give room to a man who helped a woman into her coat.

"Listen, Mal, I have to go," Tom said before Theo could answer my question. He looked a little uncomfortable. Angry. Both.

My attention pulled my date's way and I frowned. "What? Now?"

Now that we had dinner and we were supposed to have sex? Now when my panties were wet?

Theo leaned in a little. "Diarrhea," he whispered, thumbing over his shoulder toward the bathroom.

Tom flushed redder than his hair. "God, shit. Fuck, I mean, not shit. Listen, I had a nice time and all, but I can't um... yeah."

He gave Theo a quick glance, then fled.

I stared out the glass entry doors and watched him disappear. Theo didn't say anything, just seemed to be waiting patiently as I processed being abandoned by my date.

"Did that just happen?" I asked.

Out of the corner of my eye, Theo shrugged.

I turned to face him, smacked his arm. "I can't believe you just told me he had diarrhea. You might be a doctor and all and talk about bodily functions all day long, but he must be mortified. Especially since you ran into him in the bathroom. He's never going to talk to me again because of that alone. I mean, if it was reversed and that had been me, I'd literally move to another state. It's that mortifying."

I blanched at the possibility. I'd done some crazy stuff, but not *diarrhea on a date.*

"It's just a loose, watery bowel movement that can be explosive. He just needs to eat more fiber."

My mouth dropped open. How could a guy so hot be so... blasé?

I spun around and aimed for the front doors. I had to get out of here and away from men with random facts about weird shit. Literally, shit.

"Are you serious right now?" I asked when I discovered he followed.

"Aren't I always?"

Yes. Yes, he was.

"Did you drive yourself here?" he asked, following closely. Clearly, he wasn't going to apologize.

"Yes," I replied on a huff.

"I'll walk you to your car." He snagged my coat from my arm, and I had no choice but to stop so he could help me into it. "Come on."

"Why were you standing there anyway?" I asked, shifting topics. Tom was long gone and wasn't coming back. Not tonight and probably not ever.

"I came out of the bathroom behind your date, and I saw you. It would've been rude not to say hello."

That was nice. And true.

"Yes, but why are you here?" I waved my hand around the parking lot indicating The Lodge.

"I've heard you run into people all the time in small towns."

"That's your answer? Do you always have to be so vague?"

He shook his head, his dark gaze meeting my eyes, then dropping to my mouth. "Bridget told me about the place, and I thought I would get carry-out. I'm not much of a cook," he admitted, following me closely as we cut through the parking lot.

With the time change that had recently happened, it was already dark, but the restaurant had plenty of outdoor lighting.

I stopped in front of my car and reached in my purse for my keys.

"Were you going to have sex with him?"

My head whipped up, keys forgotten.

"What?" I stared at him wide eyed, his question bold. And intrusive.

He crossed his arms over his chest. Ones I now realized wasn't inside a coat. He only wore a dress shirt and dark pants, something similar to what he wore for my appointment the day before. The night was chilly and would dip below freezing, yet he didn't look cold at all.

In fact, he looked hot. As in H.O.T.

"You said yesterday Bridget fixed you up on a date with a fellow teacher and that you're going to have sex with him," he reminded.

"I... um, yes." What use was lying? He knew. "Except with his... um, bathroom problems, it probably wasn't going to happen. He did go twice during dinner." I thought back to every weird sign from the meal. Did I give him the shits? No. Not unless it was like the norovirus that swept through the middle school last February and took out almost all of the students and staff. I felt fine.

This was a date, not norovirus. If he didn't want to go out again, he could have just said, *thanks, but no thanks.* Or *I don't like women who can't appreciate Sherman's March to the Sea.*

Whatever. But diarrhea? That was quite an excuse to bail.

Was I that bad of a date? I ran my tongue over my teeth then I reached behind me and patted my butt.

"What are you doing?" he said, his gaze following my actions.

"Making sure I don't have bad breath, or the back of my dress isn't tucked up in my underwear like that one time when I was five."

He frowned. "You're fine. Completely fine."

Theo looked at me, then scanned the parking lot, as if searching for Tom and if he was going to return.

His dark gaze finally met mine. "Did you see the OBGYN referral yet?" he asked, giving me mental whiplash.

"No. I have an appointment Monday."

He nodded once. "Then you aren't personally protected from pregnancy."

I could feel the heat rush to my cheeks. "What does this have to do with–"

"You said you didn't want to have kids."

He sure listened.

"I don't. I definitely don't." No way was I bringing a child into my fucked up family. "It doesn't matter anyway," I said on a sigh. "He's clearly not here to fuck me now."

I thought I had a good shot at it. Attractive guy. Interested, or so I thought. Pretty yellow underwear to get him the rest of the way interested.

Theo's gaze dropped and raked over my body. Slowly, thoroughly. I tried not to squirm, unlike the day before on the exam table. Like then, I had to wonder if he could see through my clothes. At least this time I had panties and a bra.

"You want sex. I'll give it to you."

Bomb dropped.

"Whaaaaaaaaaaat?" I practically shouted. Had I heard him correctly. I glanced around to see if anyone else caught it because I thought I was wrong, but then to make sure this crazy convo couldn't be overheard. "I don't want... pity sex."

"What the hell is pity sex?"

"When you do it only because you want to make the other person feel better."

"I'll make you feel good, there's no doubt."

9

THEO

"You want to... to have sex with me," she said after staring at me for a while. Her voice took on a breathy quality that made my dick hard. As if it was a surprise, or a really good idea, or both. Usually, Mallory let every emotion show, or be heard. Now? I didn't know exactly what she was thinking. Or what she'd do next, which might include kneeing me in the balls.

So yeah, she made me really fucking hard.

Yes, I got a hard-on from Maude. That had been biology in action. Maude usually pulled her scrubs and panties down and bent over the break room's sink if we were going to fuck. Our relationship didn't go much further than a doctors-with-benefits arrangement. Any guy's dick would get hard for an upturned ass and bare pussy.

But this wasn't the same thing.

I had chased a reckless patient down to a restaurant

bathroom to ask after his STD covered dick and reminded him to keep it to himself for awhile. Then I asked why he was at the restaurant, if his date–and anyone else he'd slept with recently–knew he was contagious and yeah, he got the idea. It showed well for the Hunter Valley school system that one of its teachers was so smart.

I was standing in a dark parking lot and propositioning a twenty-four-year-old. It sounded bad, but in reality, it was one of the... *rightest* things I'd done in a while.

Had I thought any of this through? No. Was I thinking with my dick instead of my brain? Yes.

Because of that, all I could think of was that Mallory was the biggest fucking cock tease I'd ever met. The worst part? She had no idea. Ever since I met her back in July, when Mav first started dating Bridget, I'd been hot for her. All the things that weren't taught in medical school. I lusted. Craved. Hyper-focused. On her long blonde hair. Her pale eyes. Her full lips that would look perfect wrapped around my dick.

Her sass, which would be tamed by... you guessed it, her lips wrapped around my dick.

I sounded like Mav, that she was too young for me. I didn't care.

She was too sweet and a fucking ray of sunshine. I didn't care.

I wanted to get her all filthy. I'd wanted that since July, but now that I knew she was a virgin except for two pumps of a teenage dick, I wanted her to be the student instead of the teacher. I'd show her all the things and none of them would be G-rated.

"Yes." I reached out–I couldn't resist–and stroked a

knuckle down her cheek. I could barely see the blush that stole over her soft skin. I shifted my gaze to hold hers. "But not right away," I continued, my voice getting deeper. "You'll get the appropriate birth control method for your body and lifestyle and have it take effect first."

She blinked and her mouth opened and closed like a fish out of water. "Theo, I–"

"In the meantime," I continued on as if she hadn't started talking. "I'll give you what you need without penetration. At least with my dick."

"Theo–"

"You were going to have sex with a guy you barely know. You know me."

"Really? I've been around you a handful of times and you barely talk."

She didn't move away from my touch, which was a good sign. She wasn't scared of me. In fact, I'd swear she was just as interested. This would be a mutually beneficial arrangement.

"I'm safe. I would never hurt you." She had to know that, at least.

Her tongue darted out, ran over her lower lip.

"Mav and Dex would kick your ass if you did," she stated.

"I have a feeling you could do that all by yourself." She was a little thing, barely coming up to my chin, but she was feisty. She and Bridget were best friends, equally strong women, but Mallory seemed to have a backbone of steel. She seemed to have her shit together and didn't lean on anyone. Tough.

She grinned and I saw that sly gleam in her eye. "Absolutely."

"I know your secrets," I admitted.

Her eyes flared wide, probably realizing I was referring to her sexual history. What other secrets was she keeping?

"Are you blackmailing me?" She stepped back and I reached down and snagged her hand.

"Fuck, no. What I mean is, I know you're not experienced. I don't hold it against you or revere it. But you want sex and are willing to do it with a blind date. With me, no hard work necessary."

"You mean I'm easy," she snapped.

I shook my head and quietly let out a sigh. "No, woman. I'm easy. Me and my dick are sure things. No dating. No commitment. Just sex."

When she didn't move, I let go of her hand and slid a finger up her arm. Her jacket was thick, and she probably didn't feel much, but she was watching the path. Even held her breath as I reached her shoulder, then worked my way back down the center of her chest where her coat wasn't zipped.

"I've never... *ever* been propositioned like this." She shook her head. "No, this isn't a proposition. You're offering me a service. A stud service. Do you do this for all the women who come to you for a pelvic exam?"

"You're being insulting." I cocked my head and studied her. "To me, but more to yourself. I'm thinking maybe a spanking to curb that sass." I studied her closely. As a small town first grade teacher, she wasn't very worldly. She also didn't know much sexually, so I was definitely pushing her boundaries. But I wasn't going for basic missionary here. I wanted to find out what made her hot. Or not. Because whatever her kink, whatever her need, I'd give it to her.

Her eyes widened at that, but she didn't say anything.

"No, spanking isn't your thing, is it? You need that mouth busy with something else, like seeing how far down your throat you can get my dick."

"Now who's insulting," she countered.

"But the way you're squirming, you like it, so it's not insulting. It's foreplay."

"Oh my God." She didn't say that in an *I want to kill him* way, but *I think my panties just burst into flames* fashion.

"It'll be a mutually beneficial arrangement. Pleasurable." I liked this idea more and more. My hand slid lower, down her thigh, to the hem of her dark dress, the one that clung to her sexy curves in all the right ways.

"Just... like that?"

She and Bridget were similar in height, but while Bridget had a lean, runner's build, Mallory was curvy. Like a fucking pin-up girl. "I'll make you come, just like that. Yes. Sometimes it'll be fast, like here in the parking lot. Sometimes I'll take my time with you. Make you work for it. Beg."

I was really starting to like this idea. Mallory was equally parts needy and naïve.

"Bbb...beg?"

My finger skated along the inside of her thigh, the feel of her soft tights giving way to... bare thigh. Bare thigh?

I pushed her dress up a little more so I could see.

She slapped at my hand. "Theo!"

"Shh... no one can see." We were between two cars at the far end of a row. While people were coming and going from the lot and the entrance, no one was nearby. "What kind of tights are these?"

"Mock garters."

Mock garters. They were tights that stopped mid-thigh but continued up in a thin strip–like garters–that joined at a waistband and–

"Fuck, yellow panties. Those are making me break my rules. I'm not sure if I'll be able to wait for that birth control to kick in. Condoms alone might have to do when I take you. But not tonight." With one hand, I took hold of the bottom of her dress and held it up so I could keep touching. That bare skin was so fucking soft. Warm. The closer I got to her center it was... damp. I had to touch her panties, find out if they were as soaked through as I thought. When I got the confirmation, my knuckle brushing against damp heat, I groaned.

"Soaked. Is that from eating dinner with Tom or standing out here in the dark with me and imagining sucking my dick until you're a good girl?"

She rolled her hips into my barely-there caress, over her panties. It was such a high school move but it was the hottest fucking thing I've ever done.

"You... have your hand under my dress and you want to talk about Tom?" she questioned. She reached down, took a hold of my wrist. Not to pull me away as I first expected, but to keep my hand where it was. "You said you were going to make me come. Right here in the parking lot." She slid her panties to the side and pressed my fingers against her. Dripping wet, silky soft, and hot. "Or are you all talk?"

So much for naïve.

10

MALLORY

HE SURPRISED ME. But then I surprised him right back. I was an almost-virgin, but I wasn't clueless. I heard what my friends did. I saw movies. Porn. Read romance. Had a vibrator. So when the idea of us having sex got sorted in my brain, I was all in.

Was I going to say no to Theo James? Heck, no.

He pressed me into the side of my car and took over, tucking my panties to the side and petting me with his fingers. Gentle strokes coaxed my slit open, spreading my wetness everywhere. He found my clit. Of course he did. Within three seconds, in the dark.

"Yes, make me come," I breathed, then whimpered and rolled my hips.

"Shh," he whispered, leaning in close so his breath fanned my neck. "I'll make you come, but those sounds are for me."

When one finger circled my entrance, another sound slipped out.

"You want to be caught?"

I was so wet, it slid right in. I went on my tiptoes.

"That hurt?" he asked, knowing my sexual history. Clearly, he didn't know I played with toys bigger than real dicks. "Too much?"

I shook my head. "No. More."

He pulled back, added a second finger. My vibrator was super-sized, so I was used to being penetrated. Just not by a guy. And the vibrator didn't curl over my g-spot like Theo's fingers did.

Oh fudge.

"You want people to know you're getting finger fucked in the parking lot?"

My head dropped back against my car and my eyes fell shut.

I was hot and needy, more turned on than I'd ever been. The cool air felt good on my heated skin.

"Theo," I breathed.

"People are going to walk by and hear your sexy little sounds, see your hips roll and know where I have my hand."

Oh my God. He was a dirty talker. Filthy.

And I liked it.

Letting go of his waist, I grabbed hold of his wrist and held him deep, because he got another finger into me and was doing some kind of curling thing that had me losing my mind.

I tried to pull and push his hand, to get it to do what I wanted.

"Ah, ah," he said, stilling. I blinked and opened my eyes, suddenly furious.

"Don't stop!"

He grinned. Actually grinned. I didn't remember seeing him ever do that before. But it was sinister, as if he had dastardly plans... for my pussy.

"You're not in charge. Let go of my arm and hold your dress up for me."

He stared. I stared. This was one hill I didn't want to die on. I'd let him win this fight because well, I'd get a man-made orgasm.

I took the bunched-up edge from him and held it about my waist. If anyone walked by–

"Anyone walking by would see you holding your dress for me. So I can get both my hands on this perfect pussy." He had talented fingers and was also a mind reader.

He did have both hands on me. Two fingers buried deep doing something magical and ruthlessly talented, the other hand's thumb on my slick clit and circling it.

"They'd see you coming so pretty. You're going to come for me, aren't you? Right about..."

I squirmed and rolled my hips. Gripped my dress and clenched down on his fingers. I'd never felt like this, never knew it was even possible. I was sweating in the cold air, breathed in Theo's spicy scent, felt safe and protected, even with his words threatening exposure.

I was a first-grade teacher. So many people knew me through the elementary school. It would be so bad if I was discovered like this.

Except I didn't care because I was going to come.

"...now."

I did. I clenched and squeezed Theo's fingers and rode his hand. Whispered whimpers slipped from me. It was the best I could do because white lights danced behind closed eyelids.

I didn't remember my name let alone this was so, so naughty.

Theo kept talking to me through my pleasure, although I had no idea what he was saying. I couldn't process anything except how he'd masterfully taken control of my body.

And I liked every minute of it.

Even when he slipped his fingers from me and licked them clean.

11

THEO

"Did Verna tell you about Saturday?"

"Dr. Jeffries," I said, turning at the question. I just came from one of the exam rooms and a woman with eczema.

The older man cocked his head and gave me a look. "I've told you more than once to call me Jeff."

"I can't believe your mother named you Jeffrey Jeffries," I said, tucking the work laptop I'd had with me in the patient visit under my arm.

He laughed. I was coming to learn he was just as upbeat and warm as his wife. It took me less than an hour to know that while he and I were the practicing physicians, Verna ran the place.

I learned he was sixty; Verna told me all about his surprise birthday party last November. He had hair as white as his big smile, both a sharp contrast to his dark skin.

"Well, it makes nicknames easy," he replied. He had the laid-back attitude of a Hunter Valley local where rush hour didn't exist, and no one was a stranger. Nothing seemed to faze him, and he was always smiling, which I found somewhat annoying. How could anyone be that happy all the time?

"What's Saturday... Jeff?" I asked.

"I told you about it this morning," Verna called down the hall. She was at the front desk but had all-hearing ears. They were probably honed from wrangling their four now-grown children. No doubt she had an eye in the back of her head, too. "You just hadn't had your coffee yet."

"Probably true." Not probably, definitely. I hadn't slept very well after tucking Mallory into her car after I made her come all over my hand. Why? Because I had a hard-on that wouldn't quit. I jerked off not once, but twice in the shower and my dick still wouldn't go down. I thought of that bold, reckless woman. She'd actually wanted me to get her off in the parking lot. I should've expected it, knowing her personality, but after I learned she didn't have any sexual experience, I figured she'd want a bed to kick things off.

But no.

Fuck, she'd felt amazing beneath my hands. Now I knew how she looked when she came. How she sounded when she tried to stifle her pleasure. It was almost a shame she had to keep quiet. I didn't think she'd be a quiet lover. Hell, she wasn't a quiet person.

"Didn't help," Verna called again. This was my fourth day on the job, and she seemed to know my moods. Although to her, there only seemed to be one.

Her husband fought a smile but didn't win. "You are surly."

Surly? Try horny.

Okay, so I had two moods.

I arched a brow and didn't argue because I *was* cranky today. More than usual because I was never quite this agitated. Turned on. Needy.

Coffee from Steaming Hotties wasn't going to solve the problem. Mallory would. Getting her alone. With a bed. A couch could work in a pinch. Her naked. Or partially naked. Definitely her on her knees.

Fuck, I was obsessed with her kneeling before me.

I dropped my arms and set the laptop–again–in front of my poorly timed hard-on.

I'd been in town less than a week and had more free time than I knew what to do with. So far, I'd worked, slept, hung out with Mav and Bridget, and finger fucked Mallory in a restaurant parking lot.

My mission in life for the past fourteen years had been medicine and saving lives. Now my mission was how many different ways could I get Mallory off.

"Maybe I'm average on being surly. You and your wife could be too upbeat for your health. Ever get tested for it?"

If Mallory gave me that sass, I'd–Fuck... knees again.

He laughed because he thought I was joking. I was serious, and that made me officially surly. There had to be something wrong with serially perky and cheerful people. Like Mallory.

She was a fucking ray of sunshine. Who came like a dream. Who boldly put my hand on her pussy and pretty much called me out for being all talk and no action.

74

Oh, I took action. Her pussy had been so fucking tight. And dripping. If–no, *when*–I got my dick in there, I wasn't sure if I would last longer than the teenage one-pump chump who got there first and ruined her. Why she hadn't tried again in all those years was something I needed to figure out. There was no trauma there, not with the way she initiated and then came so quickly.

There was more to her than she let on and it seemed I could see through the cracks in her rainbow and unicorn facade. I was going to find out what made that woman tick, and scream.

Soon. Very soon, if my dick was in charge.

"—monthly volunteer fire department training."

I blinked.

"Sorry. What?"

He repeated himself. "One of us goes and participates at the volunteer fire department training."

"Meaning me."

He nodded. "Our granddaughter has a softball tournament in Missoula so it's your turn. It's important to work closely with the rescue crew and other resources. I'm sure you'll enjoy using your emergency skills and they'll be thrilled to have someone with your background. Besides, you need to meet people, make new friends."

Make friends? I wasn't nine going off to a new school or summer camp. I steered clear of that and said, "I dealt more in gunshots and multi-car pile ups than avalanches and bear attacks."

He tapped his chin, in deep thought. "Hasn't been a bear attack around here in... oh, eight years."

"Ten," Verna shouted.

"As for an avalanche, I'll tell the ski patrol leader that you're eager to take their first class this winter."

I shrugged. "I'll take snow over bears."

12

MALLORY

"How was the date?" Bridge asked.

I was at the gate waiting for my flight to Las Vegas, phone to my ear. I'd been at work, then driving to the airport and hadn't had a chance to catch up with her until now about her arranged date with Tom. Plus, Bridge had been on a plane herself. She'd texted this morning asking if my vagina had had a workout, and since my six-year-olds were coming into the classroom, all I'd responded with was a sad face emoji. I didn't even have time to respond to my mother's text asking after the groceries.

No one sat on either side of me, but I glanced over my shoulder to see if anyone was in the row of seats that backed up to mine. All clear. I wasn't having a usual conversation with my bestie where people could overhear. Who knew what we were going to say?

My college friends, Alana, Megan, and Lia, left from

Boise and Seattle and were already in Vegas. Alana, who was getting married in Mexico on New Year's Eve, sent a photo of the three of them lounging by the hotel's pool earlier and I'd been jealous. I'd been lucky though and found a cheap flight that left after school was over today so I only had to take one day off. I'd be with them by the pool tomorrow soaking up that warm sunshine.

"Not great," I replied into my cell, remembering Tom had fled the restaurant like a sprinter off the mark.

"What's wrong with him?" she wondered. "Bad breath? Did he order something with garlic? Bad kisser?"

"No garlic. I don't know about the kissing. We didn't get that far."

I wondered how much to tell her. I certainly wasn't going to mention the diarrhea. She had to work with the guy. As for Theo's presence, I didn't want to share that either because what we did in the parking lot? H.O.T. But even I couldn't explain what that had been.

If a little finger fun was all I ever got from him, I didn't want it to be awkward for Bridge. She was marrying into that family someday.

"He didn't even kiss you?" she sounded insulted for me. As if the two of them had made a plan at school and he hadn't followed through.

"No. He said goodbye to me at the restaurant."

"That's it?"

"That's it." *With him.*

"Hmm. Did he talk about the Civil War through dinner? I told him not to do that." So they had chatted.

"No Civil War talk. Just... no connection."

Not like I had with Theo, although half the time I

wanted to whack him upside the head and half the time I wanted to climb him like a monkey.

"Mmm, yeah. That won't work. When I get back, I'll see if I can get anything out of Tom."

Since they worked across the hall, I had no doubt she'd do some asking, especially if she advised him on topics to avoid in advance. He wasn't going to say anything about the date. I was absolutely positive about that. At this point, I wanted to forget about it, too.

How could I be interested in Tom after Theo and his magic fingers? I didn't know how long it took him to get me to come, but it wasn't long. Like ridiculously fast. Under a minute.

Why? Because he was a filthy talker. The guy wore khakis and dress shirts and the man–when he wasn't talking about bowel problems–was lethal.

You want people to know you're being finger fucked in a parking lot?

I could still hear the deep timbre of his voice as he said that.

Did I? Want to get caught? No. But... no.

How would I know? I'd never been finger fucked *not* in a parking lot before.

Now, before getting on a plane, was not the best time to have wet panties.

"How's it going there?" I asked, clearing my throat and squirming in the hard seat.

She was already in Boston with Mav to take down her dick professor. A perk of flying a private jet.

The bitch.

"The meeting's tomorrow," she said.

"Mav must be eager, in his usual calm, cool way."

"Oh yeah. He's been wanting to rip this guy's balls off and shove them down his throat since that night at your brother's bar when he learned the truth."

I heard Mav murmuring something in the background, but I couldn't make it out. Something like, *the man's going to wish he got his PhD in French.*

I remembered that night. Theo was there. And Mav went creepily quiet and stole Bridge away.

"At a minimum, he won't be able to get a job teaching addition to kindergartners when Mav's done with him," I said, eager for justice for her.

I was all for women taking care of their own shit, but there was something about a guy like Mav, all evil lumberjack, ready to rip the man's head off for fucking with his woman.

The gate agent got on her little microphone and announced it was time to board.

Bridge laughed. "You're all so ruthless."

Mav grumbled again, then Bridge giggled.

Mav was at the top of the ruthless list, but I was right behind him. No one fucked with my bestie.

"I gotta go." I stood, grabbed my purse and the gossip magazine I picked up at the small store after security. "The plane's boarding."

"Have fun with your friends. Don't do anything I wouldn't do." Which was anything in Las Vegas because she hated the place. The people, the noise, the lights. All of it. Me? It screamed fun. Except the fun I'd been thinking about all day had been with Theo the night before. I wondered what might happen next. Had that been a random one-off? He said, '*You want sex. I'll give it to you.*'

Would he? Or had it been a spur of the moment thing, the fooling around in the parking lot? Did he have regrets? Had I done it right?

I'd come really fast. Like ridiculously quick. I assumed it'd be flattering to a guy, being so responsive, but it was also over faster than it took to walk across the lot. I hadn't really even touched him. I could've reciprocated. A hand job or a BJ or something. But maybe he wanted someone skilled. I'd have fumbled with my hands or probably gagged myself.

Gah! I was getting on a plane doubting myself. I hadn't satisfied him, obviously. But was he satisfied by what he did?

I had no clue because we hadn't talked more after he licked his fingers, then tucked me into my car and shut my door.

He hadn't said goodbye, only knocked on the roof before walking off.

I didn't even have his number. No way in hell was I getting it from Bridge either.

"I'm not that bad," I muttered, heading for the short line, trying to put sexy thoughts of Theo out of my head. That one orgasm in the restaurant parking lot and I knew I couldn't just fuck any guy. I had a pretty good feeling my vagina–and the rest of me–was only interested in Theo.

"Yes, you are. Don't get married like Lindy and Dex," she warned. "Ooh or arrested!"

Right. As if.

13

THEO

"It's stations day."

I arrived at the station at nine and was met by Mac, the chief of the volunteer fire department. As we walked through the bay area, he pointed out each fire truck and piece of rescue equipment.

"I'm sure you saw the blood donation bus."

I nodded. I couldn't miss the rig with a photo of a woman giving blood on the side of it. No one could, which meant good advertising.

"The nurses who run the bus are organized and well prepared, but the newer EMTs will practice vitals before and after someone gives blood."

He pointed out the doors to the front parking area. Cones had been set up creating a one-way path for cars, like a drive thru. "That's for car seat installation and check. Quick in and out."

I nodded again. There wasn't much to say. The guy and his crew had this well organized. With the firefighters in either all navy, with t-shirts with HVFD in huge letters across the back, or in heavy-duty bunker pants and boots, they were easy to identify.

"The real fun's happening out back." He grinned and his impressive mustache curled up at the ends. He was probably my age, maybe a little older. Rugged in appearance, as if he lifted huge fire truck tires for exercise. He had probably thirty pounds on me of solid muscle, but I could probably run farther. Which meant if there was a bear chasing us, I'd outrun the fire chief. Except he'd probably stand his ground and punch the beast in the nose.

He cut between two gleaming fire trucks and out the huge, open garage door in the back. Two totalled cars were resting in the middle of the back lot. Men and a few women, all turned out in their firefighting gear, including helmets and safety goggles, were placing emergency tools on a tarp beside each one. I recognized the Jaws of Life, an ax, and a pry bar.

"I don't get to see this side of MVAs," I commented.

"All set, Chief," a man called. His t-shirt said lieutenant on the front, although the letters disappeared as he zipped up his bunker coat. "Hey, Doc," he called to me.

I raised my hand in hello as Mac nodded in response.

"Ready to have some fun?" he asked, slapping me on the shoulder. It was a brisk morning, but perfect weather if suited up in the thick bunker gear.

"Sure."

"Good. You're victim number one. See Gant over there and he'll get you suited up."

I arched a brow. I expected to be doing some pretend resuscitation or intubating or something. "Victim?"

He nodded. "You're going into the back of that car and we're going to rescue you. We'll try not to poke you with a tool. If we cut off your arm or break your neck practicing our medical skills, you'll be able to tell us what we're doing wrong."

"If I'm going to get poked this morning, I'll give blood."

"You can do that after the training. We have thirty minutes to get you out to stay within the golden hour to ensure we can transport the patient to docs like you in time."

He referred to the immediate window of time after an emergency during which chances of preventing death by getting someone to medical care was the highest.

"The slower team buys dinner and drinks later."

The man I imagined was victim number two just finished suiting up in bunker gear and awkwardly climbing through a broken passenger window on one of the totaled cars. A wool blanket was handed in after him, then flung over his head. Since he was only a *pretend* victim it was obvious they wanted to shield him from broken glass or any other fun debris from the extrication.

The firefighters grabbed their tools, got organized and got busy. The revving of power equipment cut through the peaceful fall morning.

"Claustrophobic?" he shouted over the noise.

"Not yet, but I might be after this."

He laughed.

I was serious.

"Let me guess, a trauma surgeon's idea of fun is sharing x-rays of the worst impalements?"

Unfortunately, he was probably right. The things I'd seen, and many of the impalements were intentional, sexual and through the anus, were pretty crazy.

Instead of answering, because I figured the question was rhetorical since he already knew the truth, I countered, "And this is your idea of fun?"

My brow never went down the entire time he talked. He and I both did our best to save lives, but the difference between his kind and mine was clear. He did the real saving and I just ensured they stayed alive.

"Hell, yeah."

"Come on."

He took me over to the unoccupied totalled car and introduced me to the group as I put on the borrowed bunker gear, piece by piece. Five men and one woman. All young. Fit. Excited.

I listened as they talked through their action plan, then was helped into the car. I had to climb through the front windshield on my stomach, then slither between the two front seats, only narrowly missing losing my balls on a stick shift before settling into the back seat. The ceiling was crumpled down and it was fucking tight. Through the dirty windows I saw the team grabbing their tools. Mac stuck his head in the front window and shouted over the power generator that just kicked in.

"You good?" he asked as I settled the borrowed helmet on my head, then tugged the safety goggles down from the brim.

"I'll buy the entire crew food and drinks if they get me out of here in under fifteen minutes."

He grinned and handed me the wool blanket, just like the other fake victim had received. "Now's when I tell you you're joining me at my kid's school on Monday. Career day."

I took the blanket, then stilled. "What?"

He grinned and his mustache twitched. "Career day. You. Me. Monday."

"I'd rather give blood in the bloodmobile," I muttered, but he heard me.

"Why'd you become a family doc then, Doc?"

"I'm thinking I may have had a mini stroke before I said yes," I muttered, looking around at my surroundings. Totaled car, hopefully competent firefighters wielding the Jaws of Life and other ridiculously sharp and pneumatic-driven power tools. "If I say no to career day, will you still get me out of here?" I yelled, then tossed the blanket over me. I wasn't sure if he was an asshole or really fucking devious.

Make new friends, Jeff had said. Right.

14

MALLORY

"I GOT ARRESTED."

I was sitting, awkwardly in my dress–the one that I thought was sexy when I put it on the night before–on the Las Vegas courthouse steps. I had the worst case of walk of shame ever. The dark green halter dress and strappy heels only looked slutty and sad in the bright morning desert sun.

Bridget laughed in my ear. "What was it? You felt up a Chippendales dancer? Stole chips off a whale at a baccarat table?"

I didn't know what a whale was, but I didn't really care. I didn't care about much of anything right now. I was hungry, dehydrated, broke, and humiliated.

"I know! You were counting cards," she continued, enjoying her own jokes. She knew very well she was the one who could count cards.

"Prostitution," I muttered.

She laughed even more. "You? Prostitution? Good one."

I frowned at a crack in the cement step. "Good enough to be handcuffed on the casino floor, put in the back of a squad car, fingerprinted, had that fun photo taken, and put in a holding cell with a few others arrested for solicitation who I'm now social media friends with until my appointed time in front of the judge and was told my case would be bound over and had to pay bail for my release." I said that in one long rush, the worst run-on sentence ever.

She was quiet.

"You're serious."

I sighed. "I'm serious."

"You were arrested. For prostitution. Your friends, too?"

I raised my face to the sun. The past two days, the warm weather had been amazing. Now, all I wanted to do was cry. This was the worst trip *ever*.

Lindy had been here back in August, returning married to Dex without remembering it, broke up with him and lived on my couch for a week. That had turned into a happily ever after, but I didn't think this was going to have the same outcome.

"No, just me." Alana, Megan, and Lia had been at the craps table with some cute guys from Georgia and I'd gone to the bathroom. And never came back.

This morning, they were already gone. Their flights home had left first thing. I hadn't even been able to say goodbye in person. I'd been able to send Alana a text before the fingerprinting and they took my things away. I'd only just learned they'd left my suitcase at the hotel concierge for me because she'd left a freaked-out voicemail in response.

"You didn't really do it, though, right? I mean, I know you wanted to have sex with a guy and all, but this is–"

"Sh–sugar, Bridge. Of course not!" I sighed.

"Then how–"

I realized something and my eyes flew open. Panic shot through me, and I cut her off. "Please tell me Mav isn't right there. You can't tell him about this. He can never, *ever* know."

"What? No, he took Scout for a hike."

Meaning they were back in Hunter Valley. I wanted to ask what the outcome was with her dick professor, but I didn't have it in me.

I sighed. "Good. But promise me. You can't tell."

"Mal."

"I didn't tell anyone when you stole those tampons at the drug store by sticking them up your hooha."

"I was twelve, had my period and it was epic and I thought I needed three at once and I went back and left five dollars on the counter later that week. There's a big difference in vagina stories here."

"No Mav," I threatened, although I was the one stranded in Las Vegas.

If Mav knew, that meant the others would hear about it. Lindy, Dex. Silas, probably. Theo. Not that any of them would blab, but I was a flipping first-grade teacher who went to Vegas and got arrested for prostitution.

And while Theo might not have found me skilled the other night in the restaurant parking lot, I didn't think he was looking for a woman to be on the other end of the experienced spectrum either.

"I could lose my job over this," I said, dropping the big one which scared the shit out of me. There weren't tons of teaching jobs in town and if word of this got out, I'd never be employable again, even if they didn't yank my teaching certification.

"Shit. Yes, fine. No Mav. Just come home and you can tell me about it over wine and ice cream."

I stood, paced. "I can't. Bridge, I'm stuck in Vegas."

"What do you mean you're stuck? You're still in jail?"

I shook my head, but she couldn't see.

Two women came out the courthouse doors. Their names were Trixie and Annie and actually were prostitutes who'd been in the holding cell with me. They were gorgeous and sexy and really nice. Somehow–because the police officers thought I was as gorgeous as them to be considered a call girl–I'd been swept up in the same undercover raid or whatever it was that they had. High-class hookers who made more in a weekend than I made in two months. To pass the hours in the cell between the late-night arrest and our court appearance times this morning, we'd talked about everything from sex moves to lipstick colors. Boy, had I learned a lot. I even got their contact info to meet up when we had our court appearances in nine days.

On their way to an awaiting car, they gave me a wave and I offered one back, completely unfazed they were leaving jail. Jail!

Me? I was about to lose it. "No. I'm out. I went before the judge and I'm free to go, at least for now. But I missed my flight this morning and it's on that cheap airline where you have to pay for a carry-on and water and a seat belt. I have to buy a new ticket without any notice, and I maxed my credit card to pay my bail. I have something like twenty-six dollars in my wallet and I covered my parents' rent this month and... Bridge, I have no way to get home. If I ask Arlo for the money, he'll think I'm turning into my mother and *that* is something I absolutely can't do. I may have to stay here and sleep on one of my new hooker friends' couches. I don't want to ask, again, because I'm not my mother, but I'm literally stuck in Nevada."

Like the bestie she was, all she said was, "On it."

15

THEO

I was on Mav's huge sectional watching Dex's hockey game on his big screen TV. Scout was snoring on his plush dog bed in front of the fire. It was pumping out the heat and I didn't know how he could lay that close without overheating, especially with all his fur. The front door opened, and Bridge bolted from her spot beside Mav.

I heard whispers and glanced at Mav, who was sprawled low on the other side of the sectional, his socked feet propped up on the coffee table. We'd cleaned up dinner of spaghetti and garlic bread. The kitchen was clean, and I was lazy and full. I'd make it back to my little house, but I wasn't in any rush. A perfect Sunday evening, the kind I never knew existed.

Being lazy. Full. A beer in hand. Good sports on TV. Hanging with family. A fire and a dog.

Two weeks ago, I was either in the OR or sleeping in my bare, boring apartment before another long shift at the hospital. It had been the same, day after day. Patients, operations, sleep. Repeat.

"I can't believe you got conned into speaking at career day," Mav commented.

"Conned? Blackmail. I was in the back of a destroyed car trying not to succumb to claustrophobia. I didn't have much choice."

Maybe there were a few downsides to small-town life.

Mac and the crew of firefighters had that totaled car pulled to pieces well within the ten-minute window for being forced to speak at Mac's kid's school assembly. I'd been covered in a blanket and hadn't seen them at work, but they'd blown out the back window, sawed through the roof supports and opened that thing up like a tin can. A medic had climbed in and settled beside me, offering me pretend injury assessment and placed a cervical collar around my neck. She'd been following protocol and her skills were excellent. So was her lady balls for climbing inside the back of a wrecked car, pretend or on a real scene. Once the Jaws of Life had pried open the back door, I'd been carefully loaded onto a backboard and placed on a stretcher in one of the ambulances for continued mock patient care.

After I'd been freed from the straps and neck brace, Mac had transitioned the training to me being the doctor I was and the EMTs and paramedics giving me a report on the fake patient they'd just saved. I had newfound confidence in the town's emergency services.

After cleanup, we'd shifted the meal from dinner to lunch and gone to the same restaurant/bar that I went to with my brothers over the summer. After burgers and a few beers, it seemed I made friends with all of Hunter Valley Fire Department. I wasn't sure if they liked me, or that I paid.

There was no question Jeff–who'd volunteered me for that morning of fun–knew what I'd been in for. Most likely he and Verna were still laughing about it, even a day later.

"You don't even like kids," Mav reminded. "How are you going to keep an assembly of them from falling asleep?"

I titled my head and glared at my brother. "I like kids," I grumbled. I didn't really, for no other reason than I didn't know any.

"What? You?" he shrugged. "You don't."

Out of the corner of my eye Bridget and Mallory–heads close together–cut past the great room and up the stairs. Mallory didn't stop to say hi, didn't even look this way.

At the quick glimpse of her as she went by, my dick stirred. I hadn't seen her since I left her in the parking lot on Thursday in that sexy dress and fake garter tights. Oh, and little yellow panties.

I shifted lower on the couch to get more comfortable with an instant hard-on.

I'd wanted to see her since, but I wasn't going to go after her, no matter how eager my dick was. It had been sex. Or almost sex. My dick–yes, he was in fucking charge–knew the difference. Sex meant he was getting some action with a hot, wet, tight pussy. Almost sex meant some time with my hand.

"What's up with that?" I wondered, tipping my chin in the direction the women went.

Mav kept his eyes on the game and shrugged. "She was in Vegas."

I frowned. "Mallory was in Vegas?"

"Bachelorette party."

Bachelorette party?

"Why are they whispering and hiding upstairs?"

A foghorn blared from the TV, indicating a goal. While Scout had slept through Mallory coming in the house, the sound startled him awake. He stood, circled three times, then dropped back down.

I caught the instant replay. Dex had scored again. The close up of his face as he grinned and fist bumped down the team bench made my night.

"Contrary to what you might think, Bridge doesn't tell me everything," Mav said. "There are some things I really don't want to know. Like if Mal fucked a dude in Vegas."

I sat up, placed my beer on the coffee table with a little more effort than necessary.

"A dude?" I asked, my voice practically a snarl.

"Whatever. I don't need to know about her sex life." He stood, pointed at my beer bottle. "Want another?"

I nodded. He headed for the kitchen and left me alone to wonder why I was so pissed off about that possibility. Mallory wasn't mine. A little finger banging didn't mean we were getting married. Hell, I hadn't even kissed her. Based off of that alone, the fact that I'd gotten in her panties without any kissing meant it was just sex.

My dick twitched, reminding me it hadn't been sex since all the action he saw Thursday night was me jacking off in the shower, then again in bed. All Mallory and I shared was *almost* sex.

I glanced up the stairs. Were they up there right now doing a play-by-play of a wild one-night stand? I had to know because no *dude* was getting that pussy. It was mine.

16

MALLORY

"Thank you so much for getting the ticket. I'll pay you back," I told Bridge as she tugged me into the master bedroom, shutting the door behind us. She flipped a switch which turned on a lamp beside a supersized, cushy reading chair in the corner.

With a quick hand wave, she shut that down.

"No, really." I grabbed her hand, squeezed it, which had her eyes meet mine. "I *will* pay you back." *I was not my mother.*

Bridget worked as a substitute teacher. I knew exactly how much she made a day. It wasn't much. Less than me and without the good benefit package. Until she met Mav, she'd been living at home with Lindy.

Then she fell for a billionaire who rented this huge-ass house where they now lived together. She didn't have to work again. She had a flipping jet at her disposal, which I could have probably flown if I didn't want to keep my arrest a secret.

I would not–NOT–take advantage of Bridge's new situation, or even her old one.

I was not my mother.

"I know. I did it for myself, really. I was selfish," she admitted, cutting off my thoughts.

I frowned, crossed the room and dropped into the chair. Even though the massive bed was made, I wasn't sitting anywhere near where she and Mav got it on. All. The. Time.

"Selfish?" I let my head fall back. "How?"

"What am I going to do with a BFF permanently stuck in Vegas?" She plopped down on the corner of her bed, crossed her legs like my first graders on the rug at the front of the classroom.

I wanted to cry all over again.

"And..." She raised one finger. "You haven't heard what Mav did to Professor Dipshit." She lifted another. "Plus, I'm dying to know why you got arrested for prostitution. I mean, prostitution!"

She waved her arms in the air and was way too excited for the situation.

I leaned forward. "Shh," I hissed. "Will you keep it down? I don't want the guys to hear." *Especially Theo.* "Tell me about Professor Dipshit."

"Fired. Papers he stole retracted."

"That's it?"

That totally sucked. Sure, I wanted the guy fired as much as Bridge, but that was all? After all the pain and suffering and sadness and anger he put her through? I wanted him tied to a spit and slowly spun over an open flame with an apple stuck in his mouth.

"With the university," she clarified. "Legally, he didn't do anything wrong so he can't go to jail for what he did. But we can sue. We—the other women and I—are going after him in civil court. Lost income, emotional distress, defamation, and so on."

I grinned. "Mav's got ruthless lawyers, I'm guessing."

"Sharks."

I felt villainous and ruthless in the sweats I'd changed into in the hotel lobby bathroom when I'd retrieved my suitcase from the concierge. My hair was up in a sloppy ponytail and the only makeup I had on was left over from the night before. I should've cared I flew home looking like this, but I was just happy to be on the plane. Besides, no one looked all too hot on a Sunday flight out of Vegas.

"I love it," I said, with a sly smile on my face. The first one of the day.

"So tell me about your new profession," she said, shifting on the bed to get more comfortable. She was probably wishing she had a bowl of popcorn for the upcoming one-woman shitshow.

"After all you went through, we can't be done with your ordeal after two minutes," I said. She'd been expelled from MIT after being seduced and stolen from by a professor. It was a big deal, and this was very anticlimactic.

She shook her head, pushed up her glasses. "Mav and I have already been celebrating. In Boston, on the plane. Here."

A pink flush spread across her cheeks and I really didn't want to know any more details about how they celebrated.

"We're going to have a party," she added. "Get Silas up here and celebrate sometime Dex has a day or two off so he and Lindy can join."

Silas was in Denver running James Corp from the main office and Dex was in the middle of hockey season.

"Now you, the hooker. Spill."

I put my hand over my face, wanting to die of mortification all over again.

"Last night, we were in the casino," I began. "Craps. Everything was fine. I had on that cute dress."

"The green one?"

I nodded. "And the strappy heels."

"Hot," she confirmed.

"I had to pee. A guy came up to me by the bathrooms and we started talking. He was cute. Seemed nice. Asked me if I was up for a little fun."

As far as undercover cops went, he had been really good looking. If he hadn't arrested me, I'd have been into a date. But he lost that chance, the jerk. Mistaking a woman for a hooker wasn't endearing.

"I asked him what he had in mind."

Her eyes widened and her mouth fell open. "What? Why didn't you knee him in the balls?"

"Because I was trying to flirt!"

"Okay," she said, circling her hand in the air for me to keep talking.

"He said he had a room at the hotel, that he was interested in a blow job, or straight sex."

Her eyes bugged out behind her glasses. "And that wasn't a warning sign? I mean, I'm all for you having a one-night stand, but maybe his name would have been good? A drink at the bar first? And what's with *straight* sex? Who has *straight* sex?"

If Bridge was asking that, then not her. Which meant she and Mav did all kinds of hot, kinky stuff. I hadn't even tried straight sex yet.

I was hurt. Wounded. I felt... like a little kid. Inexperienced and left behind. "I got caught up on the fact that he wanted to have sex with me. *Me!*"

I stood, paced in front of the huge window that overlooked the entire valley.

"Why wouldn't he want to have sex with you? You're smart and hilarious and in that dress, gorgeous."

I turned, rolled my eyes. "I'm me! Miss Almost-Virgin. Tom wasn't all that interested." I left out the stomach problems from the date. And Theo. And Theo's fingers.

"Then what happened?" she asked.

"He said he'd give me a hundred. I couldn't believe it, one because he wanted to have sex with me–"

"We need to work on your self-esteem issues."

"Says the woman who didn't think her brain was good enough for a billionaire hottie," I countered.

"Yeah, well, I got that billionaire hottie and that magical dick of his, so it's your turn to get your head on straight. You're amazing and guys want in your pants all the time!'

"Oh yeah? What guy?"

"Tom."

I shook my head. "Tom's out. There is no line of men waiting to have sex with me, Bridge. None."

"Fine, so you were stunned a guy in Vegas wanted to jump your hot bod."

"Exactly. I got all sassy and said I was worth more than a hundred dollars."

She raised her arm. "There you go! You're totally worth more than that. You've got a high-price pussy."

I nodded. "Exactly. Jokingly, I told him I was high-class and I only go for a thousand."

She groaned. "Oh God. Having the big picture, that was probably a bad idea."

"You think?" I countered.

"Shit, Mal. Your sass gets you every time."

"I know!" I threw my hands up in the air. "Has your flirting ever got you arrested? Because mine has."

She cringed because I definitely sank to an all new low.

"After that, I'm being handcuffed and read my rights, arrested for solicitation." I dropped back into the chair. "Bridge, it was mortifying."

"Is it like in the movies?" she wondered.

"Being arrested?" I stared at her for a second and realized she was serious. "Walk of shame in a big, fancy Vegas hotel full of people? Mortifying. Handcuffs? Not sexy like you might think. Pat down by a beefy woman? Let's just say I'm never switching teams."

"All those people who witnessed your walk of shame think you're a sex goddess. Ever think of that?"

I gave her a look. "Really? That's what they were thinking?"

"Fine, they were probably all judgy and thinking you're a ho. Again, it's kind of flattering."

"Trust me, it wasn't flattering. Not any part of it." I'd already relived all the late-night fun over and over. "Except my mug shot is better than my driver's license photo, so that's a perk."

"I want to see it."

"Hell, no."

"You said you had to pay bail?"

I nodded. "I had no idea you could put it on a credit card. I thought I had to deal with a shady bail bondsman named Carl or something."

"Your friends couldn't get you out?"

I shook my head. "Since they were at the craps table, they didn't see me get arrested, thank God. At the booking center, I was able to leave Alana a message before they took my belongings away, let her know what happened."

"You swiped your credit card and got out of there?"

I shook my head again. "No one gets out until a hearing before a judge. She set bail."

"That means you have to go back?"

I nodded. "I have a court date next Tuesday. Bridge, if I'm found guilty, it'll be a misdemeanor and I'll have a record. I can lose my teacher's license and my job and–"

She raised a hand, cutting me off. "That's not going to happen. Sharks for lawyers, remember?"

I shook my head. "Those are Mav's people. I can't let him help. Not only because I don't have the money to pay for them, but no way can he know about this."

"This isn't like your mom being her usual lazy self and you covering their electric bill."

"It *is* exactly the same. I did something stupid, and I won't have someone fix it for me."

She sliced a hand through the air. "Unless you're planning on being arrested again, it's not the same at all."

I pursed my lips. Considered, then shook my head. "It doesn't matter anyway. Mav can't know."

"Why not? It's kind of funny." Her lips twitched.

I glared. It was *not* funny. "I could lose my *job*. The less people who know about this, the better chance of it not getting around town. Maybe even from gossip alone."

"Mav's not going to tell people." Her tone indicated she was a little hurt I'd even consider him to lack the integrity needed to keep this secret.

"I trust him, but the less who know, the better. Even now, there's an arrest report out there. Anyone could look and find out what happened. *That* is not gossip."

"Okay, that's bad."

"I have to find the money to fly back and pay a lawyer to represent me, then hopefully get the charges dropped. That's the best scenario. Me being broke, but no longer a ho. I'll be happy with that at this point. Broke and unemployed would be *really* bad."

Then I'd *really* be my mother.

She gave me a pitying look. "I'm glad Mav suggested putting that down payment money into investments so it would grow, but now it's locked up."

I shrugged, because it was true. Mav knew about me and that house and put me in touch with one of his financial advisors. They'd promised a huge growth on the savings, and I'd been game. But that meant no touching, even now when I could use some of it. It was good in a way, that my down payment I had so far was safe. But I wouldn't be able to add much more right now.

"So much for buying that cute house you want, right?"

My stomach dropped and it was the first time all day I

felt close to crying. I swallowed hard. "Right. I'm not sure how I'm going to swing adding more to the down payment fund now. This is going to set me back months, at least."

She stood. "For tonight, you're back home. That's a start. Want to spend the night?"

I nodded. I was exhausted and in no mood to drive to my apartment.

"Pick a bedroom, then come down and watch Dex's game. Maybe we'll see Lindy on TV like last week."

I shook my head. "All I want is a shower, then sleep. I have to work in the morning, so I'll be out of here early to go home and change."

"Sure. And don't worry about the guys. I'll tell them something besides the truth."

Them. Not just Mav, but Theo, too. I could only imagine what he'd think of this. That I was either an idiot or a ho. Or both. I went down the hall to the farthest extra bedroom and laughed at myself.

Me. A ho. Had I really been arrested for being a prostitute when I really hadn't ever had sex? How ridiculously ironic was that?

17

THEO

BRIDGET CAME DOWN AFTER A WHILE, snuggled right into Mav's side to watch the last period of the game. No Mallory.

I didn't say anything, just kept my gaze on the game.

Mav didn't ask what was up with Mallory, only kissed the top of his woman's head.

Didn't he want to know what the fuck was going on?

I did.

Ask, dammit. Be fucking nosy!

I waited two game penalties, five minutes on the time clock and a commercial break when Mav got up again for another beer and a glass of wine for Bridget.

"Mallory have a good time in Vegas?" I asked, trying to sound conversational instead of probing.

She shifted on the big couch and faced me.

"Yup."

"That's all?" I asked, instead of what I wanted to get

from her, *"Did that good time involve fucking anyone with that untried pussy of hers?"*

Bridget pushed her glasses up as she shrugged. "You know the saying, what happens in Vegas stays in Vegas."

She had a good point. I'd been there before, and we'd done some shit that was probably pretty tame in comparison to others. Still, I didn't need it to be rehashed. Except she was pretty much telling me that something happened without telling me something happened. Because if Mallory hung out at the pool and drank, gambled some and saw a show, then Bridget would have just said that. No one pulled the *What happens in Vegas* line unless there was alcohol poisoning, a bad tattoo, or a wedding you didn't remember.

Like Dex and Lindy. So something fucking happened. Knowing Mallory had a get-laid goal, it was probably that. Which pissed me off. Yeah, I was a fucking hypocrite since I wasn't a monk or a virgin. But Mallory? She had me all kinds of fucked up, all because she came so beautifully on my fingers.

I appreciated Bridget's loyalty to her friend to keep secrets, but she wasn't helping.

Fuck this. I stood. "Bathroom."

"No more diarrhea?" Bridget asked with a sly smile.

"Pretty sure that problem is resolved."

Tom was history. Ha! That was fucking funny. But there was nothing I could do about a *dude* from Vegas or my anger toward him for touching what was mine. Hopefully *he* stayed in Vegas, too.

I crossed paths with Mav on his way back to Bridget. I waited at the bottom of the stairs for the couple to settle back into the couch. They were lying down and I couldn't even see them over the tall back. The game was still going, twelve minutes left, so I had time.

Good. I snuck up the stairs and headed right for Mallory. I wanted answers. And my hands on her body.

18

MALLORY

I CAME out of the steamy bathroom and froze. There, leaning against the bedroom wall, was Theo. My heart kicked into overdrive and my fingers instinctively clenched the top of the towel. For him, he was dressed down in jeans and a plain, white, long-sleeved t-shirt. His arms were crossed over his chest, completely relaxed, as if waiting for a woman to come out of the shower was natural.

Maybe it was for him.

Me? Not so much. Especially when I was naked except for a towel. I startled and a thrill shot through me. Goosebumps rose across my damp skin and not from the cooler air.

"Theo," I breathed. He was so intense, so... focused. On me.

His gaze raked down me, shoulder to bare toes and

back. I could only imagine him using that when assessing a patient, but his gaze wasn't clinical. It was hot.

My nipples hardened and I gripped the towel even tighter.

"Have fun in Vegas?" he asked, his voice deep, even. Low. I had to wonder what his resting heart rate was because the man was *chill*. It made sense, being a trauma surgeon and all. His profession required a level head, a steady hand, and a calm demeanor.

Out of those three, I liked his steady hands the best.

"Sure," I replied, a little wary as to why he asked. Bridget wouldn't have gone downstairs and blabbed. Not unless Mav decided to tickle the answer out of her. Or orgasm denial. I heard it was a great persuasion tool, although I wouldn't know. "What are you doing in here?"

The door was closed behind him, meaning he hadn't wandered in lost.

"I think you know the answer."

Yup, definitely not lost.

"Oh?" My heart was galloping faster than a horse at the Kentucky Derby. "What's that?"

He ran a finger over his new beard which was a little longer than Thursday night. It made him look less like a stuffy doctor and more... rugged. And dangerous, because he was impossibly more handsome. More intense. More fiercely male. More everything.

Which meant I felt more. More sizzle. More heat. More heart clutching need.

Why him? Why this man who seemed to have Superman vision and knew I was wet and aroused? He must have pheromones seeping from his pores. Why else could I always be so affected by him? Right from that first glimpse of him in the photo on Mav's laptop I'd been drawn in.

"Sex."

That one word had everything in me clenching. *Sex. Yes, please.*

This wasn't the restaurant parking lot, and I should be used to Theo's direct ways by now.

"I haven't gotten the prescription for birth control yet," I reminded. He'd been so adamant last week about protecting me from not only STDs but pregnancy.

He pushed off the wall and came closer. I swallowed, held my ground. I wasn't afraid of him, but what he made me feel.

"I know," he replied. "You said your appointment's this week."

He remembered, but then again, I had no doubt any guy would keep track of when he could get his dick inside a woman.

"Tomorrow."

His dark eyes were on my thighs, as if he remembered how they looked and felt beneath his palms. "There's lots of different kinds of sex. Did you like coming on my fingers?"

I licked my lips. Nodded.

I wasn't a prude. Or shy. Or a liar. He knew I'd liked it by the way I came. If speed orgasms were an Olympic sport, I'd be a gold medalist.

"This time, you'll come on my mouth."

Oh my go–sh. My pussy clenched again, and my hard nipples chafed against the damp towel.

Speaking of damp...

He stepped even closer. Oh, fu–dge.

"Lose the towel."

19

MALLORY

I HAD no idea why Theo made me nervous. No, I did. It was simple. It was because he was Theo James. Everything about him made me come alive. My heart accelerated, and my breathing turned into breathy little pants. My hands got sweaty. My pussy clenched.

It made no sense. The guy was quiet. Sullen, even. Moody. He was a highly educated professional, yet he'd moved here to Hunter Valley. He was a total fish out of water.

He was my complete opposite.

He was older. Completely different career. Worldy.

Especially because there was no doubt he was experienced in *all* the things.

Like right now.

Lose the towel.

He was in control. He knew what he wanted and that was to make me come. With his mouth.

On my pussy.

I'd never had a guy do that to me before. Now *I* was the fish out of water. I wasn't–

Shut up, Mallory! The guy wanted to eat me out and I stood around like an idiot.

He patiently watched me, waited. His gaze was heated, needy. His stance confident. His words... gah. Panty melting, if I were wearing some.

If he could make me come like he did in the parking lot, I was all for it.

So I dropped the towel.

20

THEO

SHE DID IT.

She dropped the towel.

Holy fuck, she was gorgeous. Short and curvy, her skin so pale I could see a network of light blue veins beneath. Her wet hair clung to her shoulders, droplets of water sliding over her, leading my gaze to her full breasts, perfectly lush and rosy tipped.

Tucked away behind a closed door in the back corner of Mav's house, she was all mine. I licked my lip with an eagerness to get a taste of her.

Her hips were wide, plenty to hold onto when I fucked her. At the apex...

"You're bare."

She looked down at herself, shook her head. "I've got a little landing strip. I think completely bare's a little weird."

"A triangle pointing to the promised land," I clarified.

My dick strained against my jeans to get to it.

She flushed because if she'd never had a man between her thick thighs before, then she didn't understand just how perfect that pussy was. And I only got a hint of pink folds.

I approached, set one hand on her shoulder and the other boldly over her pussy, cupping all that hot, damp flesh.

She startled but didn't move. Her eyelids drooped and her hips rolled into my palm.

"Wet," I said, stroking over her folds.

Her eyes fell closed and her mouth opened, her warm breath fanning my neck. This close, I couldn't miss her sweet scent. Whatever shampoo was in the bathroom, but also the musky hint of her arousal.

She was potent, which meant dangerous. I wanted her to be on birth control, but condoms alone worked. Now that I had my hands on her, I wasn't sure if I could wait. Condoms alone wasn't irresponsible... No.

Her hand took hold of my wrist, pressed me more firmly against her. Not shy, just... new. The way she'd clenched so responsively around my fingers when she came last week, her untried pussy would milk the cum from my balls once I got inside her.

I groaned, realizing she was different. I'd never felt such attraction and need before. Not only to get off, but to get *her* off. My dick was staying–sadly–in my pants and it didn't matter. My goal was to get her to come. I'd eat her out, get her arousal and need all over my face.

Fuck, yes. The idea of having her pussy scent in my

beard and her taste on my tongue... I growled, feeling ridiculously possessive.

"Theo," she whispered, her hands going to my biceps to hold on.

Leaning down, I took a nipple in my mouth, gave a hard pull. Her hands shifted to my hair, tangled and tugged.

I alternated between those perfect mounds, discovering she liked it a little rough, a little wild. Just like she was. Her hips rolled and my name breathlessly escaped her lips when I pulled back. Inspected my work, where I saw those tips were tight and bright pink.

Dropping to my knees onto the bedroom's carpeted floor, I kissed down her belly, then nudged her center with my nose.

"Fu–dge," she murmured.

I lifted my head, stared up her perfect bare body.

Her eyes opened and she looked down at me with a confused, needy look.

The corner of my mouth tipped up. "Fudge?"

"I swear too much," she explained. "Gotta be careful around the kids."

I nipped at her inner thigh, and she gasped. "Definitely no kids here. My new goal is to get you to say fuck when you come. No, shout it."

"Theo."

I loved the way she breathed my name, as if she was right there with me, that somehow, I was hitting every one of her hot buttons.

It was time to find one more. With my mouth.

With my hands on her hips, I turned her so her back was to the bed. I shifted and with a little push between her breasts, she dropped onto the edge. Grasping her ankles, I lifted them, which had her tipping back.

Placing one foot, then the other, on the mattress, I had her wide open and the perfect view of her gorgeous pussy.

"Wait."

I looked up her body and into her eyes. There I saw a mixture of arousal and nervousness. No, confusion. Resolve? Fuck if I knew. I wasn't going to do anything she didn't want, even if her body was all in. Since the teenaged kid who took her virginity didn't do more than a few overeager pumps, this was probably pretty intense for her.

I was intense on top of that. I waited.

"Do you... I mean, are you assessing my vagina? I mean, like a doctor... um, clinically?"

What? *That* was what was going through her head?

"First off," I said, keeping my voice calm and even, knowing her concerns might be a little odd, but were valid. I saw her as a patient just last week and we would've–clinically–ended up in a very similar position if I'd completed the exam instead of referred her. "I've been in the trauma department for years, specifically in surgery. I only worked a two-month OBGYN residency rotation when I was twenty-six and I assure you, I was never once aroused. By any patient. Until you."

I stood so she could see how hard I was, how my dick was going to have a zipper mark in it from my jeans.

"During the appointment, you got hard for me?" she asked, her eyes wide with surprise.

I nodded. "I referred you to a doctor who will be professional and take care of your healthcare needs. As for me? I can't be professional with you."

"You... can't?" Her confusion was endearing. Sweet. Totally fucking hot.

"No." Abso-fucking-lutely not. I proved it by sliding a finger over her center.

"Ohhh."

"Secondly, this is your vulva and this...is your labia. Right here is your clit." She gasped at the light stroke. "*This*" –I slid a finger inside of her– "is your vagina." I slipped my finger from her, slick to the first knuckle with her arousal.

She whimpered and I continued on.

"What I'm interested in is your *pussy*, which is this." I cupped her, *all* of her.

Keeping my palm where it was, I stood, then set my other hand on the bed beside her head, loomed over her so all she could see was me. Her eyes widened and she was so fucking pretty.

"And Mallory, I *love* pussy."

I watched her throat work as she swallowed hard. A flush crept down her skin, so pretty. Everything about her was so blatant. So open and responsive.

"Did I answer your questions?"

She nodded. "Yes," she whispered, her breath picking up.

"Good. You okay if I eat your pussy now?"

"Oh gosh." Her eyes fell closed and she took a second. Yeah, she was thinking too fucking much. "Yes."

Good. Excellent, because my mouth was fucking watering. I settled back on my knees between her parted thighs, my hands sliding down that silky skin as I went.

Instinctively, she tipped her knees inward, a sign of

unintentional modesty, but it offered none. From what I knew of this woman, she wasn't all that modest. She was a very empowered, very forthright woman. But naked and her pussy on display, she wasn't in charge, I was. She instinctively felt that power shift.

Sliding my hands back up the insides of her thighs, I held them wide, then leaned and licked from her clenching little hole to her clit, cleaning up the mess she was making. For me.

Fuck, I loved her taste.

"Oh my God," she blurted out. I smiled against her hot, scented skin. Already forgetting to curb her words. Perfect.

"Do this with anyone before?" I asked, setting a palm on her lower belly and using my thumb to pull back the hood on her hard little clit. It was swollen and right there for me to suck and flick with my tongue.

"Wh–what?"

"Ever get your pussy licked before?"

She shook her head, pretty much thrashed it from side to side.

Instantly, I felt like a fucking caveman.

Was it wrong to know I was the only one to know how she tasted, how she whimpered? Yes. But I didn't give a shit. Not when her sweet taste was on my tongue and her scent in my nose.

"Theo, please. I need more than a lick. Don't you dare fucking stop."

She begged and swore so sweetly. I grinned and I didn't remember the last time I found someone so amusing. Refreshing. Endearing. Delicious.

Reaching down, I shifted my dick in my pants. All I had

to do was slide the zipper down and I could thrust right inside her. I'd have all of her sticky sweetness coating more than just my mouth.

No. Another time. Now I'd have the perfect treat. It was time to take what was mine.

Her pussy. Her orgasms. Her moans and screams.

I flicked her clit with my tongue, rimmed her entrance with a finger. Circled both, around and around. Watched her carefully for how she tensed, gasped, melted.

Then I added a finger, pressing against her g-spot I'd discovered the week before.

By the time she was coming on my face and fingers, her thighs were pressed into my ears, her fingers tangled in my hair, her juices soaking my short beard.

"Fuck!" she cried, clenching around my finger, a glorious dousing of her arousal dripping down and onto my palm. Her clit pulsed and lengthened against my tongue, and I didn't stop. She came once. She'd come again. "This is insane, I can't believe… what was that…more, yes, don't stop."

She was uninhibited in her need. Focused on her pleasure. Mindless.

Because of me.

After I was done with her, she wouldn't even remember Tom's name or any guy from Vegas.

I didn't ease up. The opposite. I added a second finger, pressed and curled on her g-spot as I sucked at her clit some more.

"Theo, too much. Slow down, no more! Don't stop. Oh!"

Yes, my name. She knew who was between her thighs. Knew who gave her pleasure.

She was incredibly responsive, highly orgasmic, regardless of what she thought about herself. The second time she came was gentler, but intense because all her muscles relaxed except her inner walls, gushing and milking my fingers as if wishing it was my dick.

Sweaty, panting, and sated, Mallory didn't move. Didn't bring her legs together when I sat back on my heels and wiped my mouth with the back of my hand.

"I love eating pussy, Mallory," I told her.

I wanted my mouth on her some more, but I had to stop.

I'd shown her what it was like to get her pussy nice and eaten. Given her orgasms that would ruin her for anyone else. She was perfect. Her pussy was perfect. I was addicted. Possessive. I wasn't done with her. I wanted to get my dick inside her, watch her squirm and shift as she adjusted to being crammed full, but not now. Not at Mav's house.

"Fair warning." I stood, took in how perfect she was, bare and wanton, wrecked and completely ruined. Yeah, Tom was out of the fucking picture because no one would see Mallory like this but me. Because I did this to her.

Total. Fucking. Caveman.

The only thing better than the sight before me would be to see my cum dripping from her.

Soon.

I shifted my dick again, then headed for the door. My job here was done.

21

MALLORY

FROM MY SPOT at the back of the assembly room–a strategic location so parents and teachers were spaced around the room–I watched as Mrs. Fujikawa, Ethan's mom, shared with all three first-grade classes about her job as an architect. It was the annual first-grade career day, which meant the entire morning was devoted to various parents sharing fun facts about their jobs. So far we'd heard from a woman on ski patrol at the resort, a dad who ran wilderness trips, and another who was a sign language interpreter.

Ethan was the speaker's third child, so she had a knack for keeping the kids engaged.

All eighty of them were seated around a semicircle of risers completely enthralled because she just finished using a glue gun and popsicle sticks to quickly build a little bridge. As she did so, she explained how it was an architect's job to make sure it was sturdy by using triangles and math. She stopped and got the kids doing a drum roll as she placed a brick on the top to prove it.

The kids gasped and murmured in awe at how it held up. It was pretty impressive.

Regina, one of the other first-grade teachers, joined the woman at the front, thanking her for her presentation, directing the kids to share their thanks. They clapped and Ethan ran up to his mom and gave her a hug–and snagged the popsicle stick bridge to show off later.

"I'm not sure if I can top that."

A familiar voice cut through the excited chatter of all the kids.

I turned and there was Theo. Here, at the school.

I blinked, confused. "Um... hi."

His dark eyes raked down my body and took in my black jeans and Hunter Valley Elementary red sweatshirt. It had a big falcon on the front, the school's mascot. I was covered head to toe, in complete contrast to how he'd left me the night before, his mouth glistening with my arousal, his short beard coated in me.

Coated.

I'd been naked. Sprawled wantonly across the guest bed.

He'd gotten me off... twice, with an insane tongue/finger combo, then left.

No reciprocation. He'd been fully dressed, and I'd been completely bare. Legs spread wide.

After that, I'd crashed hard. The day had been hell. I

hadn't slept in jail the night before. God, jail. Seriously, I was still processing being arrested. And me, for solicitation? I hadn't even seen Theo's dick and *I* was the one having to post bail for offering sex for money.

Totally ironic.

The long trip home had been far from restful. And it seemed two orgasms were the best sleeping pill around.

But when my alarm went off this morning, reality came crashing back. As I'd brushed my teeth, I made a mental list.

1. I had to go back to Las Vegas, stand before a judge and explain that I wasn't a prostitute and why the undercover cop thought I was one.
2. I had to find the money to actually get to Las Vegas to do that. And a lawyer.
3. I had to keep all of that a secret from the Hunter Valley gossip grapevine.
4. 1-3 didn't take into account Theo and his exceptionally dedicated and focused oral skills. Or the fact that we'd never kissed. That he didn't linger after satisfying me. That he didn't seek reciprocation. I felt... serviced.

Of course, every woman in the world would be happy with being *serviced* by Theo James. He'd said if I wanted sex, it'd be him to do it with. He didn't say *date*. Or use the *relationship* or *love* words.

Even though I'd made the bold statement that I was marrying Theo–more than once–I had no silly notions

about that actually happening. I hadn't had epic
expectations from Tom either, but I did ultimately want to
find someone. Get married. Sure, I'd kept pushing that I
was going to marry Theo, but that had been loud-mouth
me. Theo didn't want marriage.

He said he was going to give me sex, without dick
penetration. Until I got on birth control. Then I'd get The
Dick. I hoped. If I got the shot at my appointment this
afternoon, the one I read up on, I'd be covered immediately.
Not that we wouldn't use condoms as well. He'd said two
forms of protection.

I didn't want kids but clearly Theo didn't either. Or he
didn't want to be tied to me.

I totally caught on to that. He might be a vigorous and
thorough lover–from what we'd done so far–but we hadn't
even *kissed*. No foreplay, although how he licked and sucked
on my nipples the night before probably counted. He was
so unbelievably hot... but distant at the same time. There
was a connection, chemistry, between us. But no
attachment.

Beneath my plain bra, the nipples he'd worked over so
well the night before now tingled. Good thing the
sweatshirt was loose because he'd see how hard they were
otherwise. Same with everyone else in the assembly
room.

"Whatever you're thinking, I want to do to you later," he
said, leaning in close, not that anyone could overhear.

I flushed. I could feel the heat on my cheeks, and I was
sure I was as red as my sweatshirt. My mind just went on a
trip somewhere inappropriate for being in a room full of
first-graders.

With a quick throat clear, I asked, keeping my voice just above a whisper, "What are you doing here?"

Theo leaned against the wall and tipped his chin toward the front of the room where the fire chief was presenting. "Mac pretty much blackmailed me into participating." He didn't sound that thrilled about the idea, especially since it took coercion to do it.

"You know Mac?"

He nodded. "Firefighter training on Saturday."

"Ah." I didn't know how Mac had blackmailed Theo, but he didn't seem to be in the mood to share.

The kids clapped for whatever Mac just said. He was in his bunker gear and held his helmet and oxygen mask up for the kids to see.

"What am I supposed to say to these guys?" Theo asked. "Mac says I have a stick up my ass."

I quirked my lips and stayed silent.

"You think I have a stick up my ass?" he prodded his eyes clearly concerned with this possibility.

"You had an intense job. A lot of responsibility. I think... I think you're serious. Focused."

I liked that focus when it came to giving me orgasms.

He was quiet, as if considering my words. I tried to be as diplomatic as possible. Compared to his brothers, he really *was* serious. Sometimes he did have a stick up his ass, but I had a feeling Mav had one too before he found Bridge. Maybe Silas did as well, but I hadn't been around him all that much. He was quieter instead of intense.

As for Dex being serious? No way.

"I have no idea how to talk to eight-year-olds," he admitted.

"They're six," I clarified.

His jaw clenched. "Six? Even worse. I deal with trauma. Bad stuff. Not learning how to interact with them and shape their small minds."

I found his concern amusing. Theo wasn't what anyone would call tender. Or sweet. Or warm and fuzzy. The way he'd abandoned me with my orgasmic haze, I'd say he wasn't a cuddler.

He seemed to really have no clue what to do with children.

"They're not off to med school tomorrow, so make it fun," I instructed. "Silly even. If you polled them, they want to either be a princess, an astronaut or a snowplow driver."

"I'm guessing no parent is a princess?"

"You're the fill in for her. Her tiara was being cleaned," I said with a straight face. "You'll do fine. Have fun, but it's always nice to throw in a reminder of how to be safe." I pointed to Mac who was on the floor demonstrating Stop, Drop, and Roll. The kids were laughing as he flailed around like an upside-down turtle at the end.

"Safe. Fun. Got it."

The ominous tone sounded more like he didn't have it at all.

I studied his profile as he watched Mac explain what he would look like during a fire so the kids wouldn't be scared before putting on his oxygen mask so they could see. He wrapped up quickly after that.

"Well, shit. He has stickers," Theo muttered as Mac pulled a stack from one of the many pockets on his bunker pants.

I bit my lip, trying not to smile.

He must've known he came next because he pushed off the wall but turned to me.

"My place, six." His gaze held mine. Direct and potent as usual, none of his kid-wariness visible. "Come hungry. I will be."

Oh fudge.

22

THEO

"Boys and girls, now that you have your stickers, settle down." Mrs. Sanchez, the first-grade teacher Mac introduced me to when we arrived, patiently waited for the room to go quiet. "It's time for Dr. James to share with us about being a doctor."

The kids clapped as I moved into the center of the amphitheater, but I could tell they were distracted by the SWAG. Why did Mac have to give out stickers? The only thing worse than going after stickers would be if he handed out puppies.

I cleared my throat. Sixty or seventy wiggly, squirmy kids sat before me crosslegged. *They* were like puppies. My mind instantly went to the boy who died on the operating table. The one whose death didn't have any emotional impact on me at all. These kids were just a little bit younger than he'd been. These kids could get in a car after school and be hurt in an accident, their vehicle totaled just like the one from the fire department practice on Saturday morning.

The boy who died had been ejected, no extraction needed, like practiced.

But these little innocent faces, completely clueless to what could happen in life, wanted to hear from me about my job.

The one that made me feel nothing.

"I'm Theo James and I'm a doctor."

The kids stared at me or stared off into space.

"Anyone got a mom or a dad who's a doctor?" I asked.

Three kids' hands shot up.

"Anyone been to the doctor?"

Pretty much everyone's hand went up.

I glanced over all the little heads and saw Mallory in the back where I left her in her cute fucking school sweatshirt. She made a funny face and tipped her head back and forth. Either she was having a seizure or giving me a reminder to make it fun.

"Everyone's been to the doctor. Good. You don't have to always see a doctor when you're sick. It's important to go to see a doctor to make sure you're healthy and stay that way. To get shots you need so you don't get a communicable disease."

Mallory's eyes went wide and stared at me like I was insane. Or an idiot. I was speaking as if I was at a conference full of boring trauma surgeons who found joy in a splenectomy at three a.m.

I just told a roomful of little kids about shots. Communicable diseases.

Clearly, I was the smartest idiot around. Mallory was right. I *was* serious. I glanced at Mac, who was only shaking his head in clear disappointment.

Holy shit. I had a stick up my ass.

I left Denver and moved to Hunter Valley so I didn't turn into—or any more into—one of my boring, monotonous colleagues who didn't engage with anyone on a real, personal level. I was standing here, in a roomful of fucking kids, because of the decision to escape and now I was behaving exactly like the person I didn't want to be.

Lighten up, James! Get your shit together. People have feelings! They want fun. Excitement. Joy.

I could be fun. I could be fucking fun all day long.

I glanced at Mac again. The fucker. No way was he and his stickers were going to be more likable than me. I was the cool doctor. I, Theo James, was cool.

And competitive.

Not only did trauma surgeons not like to lose—because that meant a patient died—but I also had three brothers, one a professional hockey player whose job was to always win.

Mac and his stickers were going down.

I pulled the imaginary stick out of my ass and tossed it aside.

"Who here has farted?" I said, my voice carrying across the big room.

Kids giggled and some covered their faces with their hands. Parents and teachers around the room gasped and stared at me wide eyed. Yup, I just went there.

A few hands went up, all boys.

"Come on," I said, moving my hand in a circle. I pointed at Mac. "I bet the fire chief farts."

His mouth dropped open and his ears turned red. He couldn't lie. Not to a roomful of kids.

"That's my dad and he farts all the time!" A kid toward the back called out, one that looked a hell of a lot like a miniature version of Mac.

Mac gave his son a dad look, then offered me a thumbs up as his answer.

"See?" I asked, then turned back to the kids. "Now don't be shy. Who here has farted?"

Some kid actually farted. Everyone laughed. I couldn't help but smile.

"The kid in the blue shirt just gave everyone an example of how amazing the human body is."

The kid blushed, but grinned and showed he was missing his top two teeth.

"Now who's burped?" I continued.

More hands went up this time.

"I bet Miss Mornay burps."

Everyone turned and looked at her in the back. It was her turn to blush, but she caught on and patted her stomach. "Every meal," she called, used to speaking up so she could be heard.

The kids burst out in giggles.

"Know what the body's doing when you fart or burp?"

The kids shook their heads, all eyes on me. Oh yeah, I had them hooked.

"You're letting excess gas or air from your body," I explained. "Like you're one big balloon. It was made to do that. Despite what your parents and teachers say about doing it in public, you're supposed to fart and burp."

The kids started talking, probably telling each other

that they'd been wronged their whole lives, so I raised my hands in the air. "That's not all," I called over the chatter.

They instantly fell silent because what on earth could I talk about next?

"What about throwing up? Vomiting. Upchucking. Tossing your cookies. Who's done it?"

Now every kid's hand was up and practically waving at me.

"One time, I threw up in the back seat of the car all over my brother," I regaled. "He had it in his hair, all over his shirt. Some even got in his ear."

Groans and laughing ensued.

I couldn't help but smile, remembering how Silas hated me for a week after that.

I held up my hands again and the kids quieted. "When you throw up, your body is getting rid of something it doesn't like. The body's supposed to get rid of stuff like air, gas, and yucky things from our stomachs. Studying to be a doctor, you get to learn all kinds of fun stuff like that."

I glanced at Mac, who was slowly shaking his head, a smile turning up his mouth.

I remembered Mallory's advice. "Now, that's stuff that comes *out* of our bodies. Let's go over things that shouldn't go in. What's bad to put in our bodies?"

All the kids called out different things. It was chaos. Mrs. Sanchez came to stand next to me. She raised her arm over her head and gave the peace sign.

Clearly that meant shut the hell up. It worked.

"Thank you," I said to her, then glanced around the group. "I heard drugs. Smoking. Cleaning supplies and I think even Legos."

The kids laughed.

"Knowing these things should stay out of your body–or that of your brothers and sisters–means you're all on your way to being doctors already. Be sure to tell your parents the next time you fart, it's healthy. Just your body working right."

The kids clapped with more enthusiasm than for Mac.

Ha.

I nodded to Mrs. Sanchez, who, by the look on her face, wasn't sure if she was afraid she was going to get seventy parents calling in or if she was thrilled to send kids home to expel healthy farts.

I met up with Mac and we headed out of the assembly room. Apparently, I was the last of the speakers and the teachers–including Mallory–were giving directions on walking quietly through the halls to recess.

"Farting?" he asked, pushing open the school's front door, shaking his head. "My kid's going to let one rip in front of his grandmother and blame it on me."

I grinned, pleased with how fun I was–stick free.

Slapping him on the shoulder, I told him, "You'll think twice about what you do with me at next month's training."

23

MALLORY

I DROVE past Mrs. Jonsdottir's house at a crawl. I did it several times a week, just to stare and dream. Just like a guy who passed a fancy sports car in a dealer's lot he desired, I pined for the little place. Mrs. Jonsdottir once shared that it had been her parents' house and they'd bought it as a kit from the Sears Roebuck store, which I found fascinating. It had come in pieces on the railroad, and they'd assembled it with instructions, just like a Lego set.

I pulled over across the street to eye it dreamily. I assumed the white clapboard siding was the original color. The older woman kept the house in perfect condition, but I knew I'd paint the porch ceiling a robin's egg blue to add more vintage flair. The two shrubs that flanked the front steps would be replaced by hydrangeas since it faced north and would be shady.

I had plans. Lots of them.

My cell rang and I grabbed it from my purse. My mother. I sighed, tossed it back in the bag, ignored. I didn't even have to wonder what she wanted.

She was a reminder that it would take longer now to get the house. I owed Bridge for the plane ticket. I had to get another one or pay for the gas to drive. And a lawyer. I would get the money for bail back if I was acquitted and that would go to Bridge. Well, if I wasn't acquitted, then I'd have bigger problems than losing that money. I'd lose my job as well. There wasn't a chance of buying from Mrs. Jonsdottir or anyone else after that.

The charges were going to be dropped. They were. They *had* to be. Like Aspen always said, use positive energy and manifest the outcome you wanted.

I wanted to buy Mrs. Jonsdottir's house. Therefore I wouldn't have a record and I'd have money to pay for it.

Positive energy. *Positive energy!*

It was so hard to be upbeat and cheery–like I was with my class of kids all day–when I had all this looming.

There was one way to forget about it all, at least for a little while.

Theo.

He'd invited me to come to his place at six. Not invited, *told*.

I pulled away and drove the few blocks to the little house Dex used to stay in but was now Theo's.

He was waiting for me in the open doorway as I came up the walk. He wore the same clothes as he had at school in what I called his doctor-wear, khakis or dark pants and a variety of crisp button ups. Now though, his feet were bare.

"All the kids could talk about for the rest of the day was

farting," I told him. "The playground monitor said it was a noisy recess."

A movement in the corner of my eye had me glancing to the right. By one of the little shrubs that lined the front of the house was a thin calico cat eating from a dish. He paused long enough to eye me warily. He went back to eating but looked prepared to bolt at any second.

"You have a cat?"

He shrugged. "Stray. He's been around and I've been feeding him. He used to run off, skittish and all, but he's getting a little better."

I stared at the cat a little longer, surprised at the gesture. "Oh."

The corner of his mouth quirked up. "You're late."

My heart skipped a beat at his serious tone, contrasting with the playfulness in his dark eyes, and it wasn't because of the cat. Why did I like that tone? That look? The way he loomed. He was intense. Everything about him was... potent.

He also felt... uncomplicated. There didn't seem to be any ulterior motive with him. He said come over at six because he'd be hungry. For me.

What he said, he meant. Compared to my mother, whose every word was passive aggressive or straight-out guilt. She knew how to work me to get what she wanted. Theo did, too. Oh, he *did*. He could work me right to an orgasm. Except he had no ulterior motive. Not even reciprocation.

He might be abrupt, but he was also refreshing. I knew where I stood with him. Right now, that was at his house to get sex. Sex he offered and I seemed content to accept.

"I stopped by the house I want to buy," I explained why I wasn't here on time, five minutes ago.

He stepped back and let me enter. "Didn't know you were looking for a place."

I set my purse down. "I found the one, but it'll be a little while." I explained how Mrs. Jonsdottir was going to eventually sell to me, leaving out why it might be delayed.

"Which house?" he asked, closing the door behind him.

"On Maple, the white Sears and Roebuck."

"Good for you. Now strip. I'm hungry and want to eat your pussy."

Back to serious. Seriously dominant.

I held up my hand. "I'm all for a voracious pussy eater, but aren't you skipping a few steps?"

He frowned, looked down my body as if trying to figure out what those steps were.

I tapped my lips. "We've never even kissed."

He moved close, stroked my hair back. I breathed in his scent. A hint of spicy cologne or body wash. "You want romance?"

I frowned. "Kissing is what you consider romance? Did you not kiss your past lovers?"

His eyes shifted from mine and glanced over my shoulder, deep in thought, which answered my question.

"Never mind. I don't really want to talk about women you've been with. I'm not asking for a proposal. Just... kissing."

"You wanted to sleep with the history teacher," he stated.

I nodded. "Yeah, I want sex, but I don't want a transaction."

"What's the difference?"

I blinked. Then again. When he waited patiently for me to respond, I realized he was serious. He really didn't know. He really didn't kiss women he fucked?

"Um, well..." What were the women like he'd been with? Hookers? That made me laugh because to the eyes of the Las Vegas Police Department, I was one. "Fun."

"Fun."

I nodded. "Fun."

"You want me to make licking your pussy fun?"

I frowned. "Isn't it? Is it a chore? Ugly? Weird or something? I've heard of meat curtains and maybe I have them. Something like hemorrhoids would be a turnoff, not that I have one or anything, but–"

He put a finger over my lips, full on smiling now.

"No guy looks at a pussy and thinks meat curtains."

"Okay."

"Your pussy isn't ugly, Mallory. Last night, I showed you how hard you get me."

"I saw a bulge," I clarified. "No actual body parts."

"You want to see my dick?" he asked, dark brow raised.

I raised one back, waited. Game on.

He grinned, as if silently saying *Hold my beer.*

Stepping back, he plucked open the button on his pants, slid down the zipper so they slid down his hips. I held my breath as he reached into the opening and beneath his boxers to pull himself out.

And there it was. Theo's really big, really hard dick.

He gripped the base in one hand, and I still saw inches of the steely length. Flared head, small slit at the top. I'd seen dicks before. Movies. Porn. Photos online. This was the first in-person one and it was impressive.

My pussy clenched in anticipation. My favorite dildo was huge, but comparable in size to Theo. Since it was called King Cock, that meant Theo was *huge*.

"See? This is for you," he said, his voice going deeper.

I'd never wanted to give a blow job before. The idea hadn't ever been that appealing. Porn usually showed a woman practically choking on it, with streams of mascara running down her face. She looked... miserable.

But Theo's dick made my mouth water. I wanted to know what it felt like against my tongue. What it tasted like.

The women I'd been arrested with, Trixie and Annie, the *actual* hookers, had given me some pointers. Sex pointers. We'd had hours stuck in lockup and conversation had been easy. I was far from introverted and could talk with anyone. However, I quickly discovered I was boring in comparison to them. There wasn't too much a first-grade teacher could share that was interesting, especially one who'd only had sex once when she was sixteen. But two high-class call girls? Heck, I'd wanted to know everything, so I asked. By the time we'd been taken to the courthouse, I'd had quite the sex education lesson.

Including how to make a man lose his mind and have him eating out of the palm of my hand. I had something else Theo could eat out, but from Annie's lessons, I understood the power a woman could have on her knees.

I lifted my gaze, held Theo's. Smiled. I was definitely game for trying out something I learned. Maybe the few hours in lockup would pay off.

"I want to put it in my mouth," I said. "Suck you."

Three things happened at once. Theo's eyes went dark and heated. His cheeks flushed with arousal and his dick grew in his grip.

"First time?" he asked, giving himself one long, slow pump.

I nodded, licked my bottom lip as a bead of pre-cum seeped from the slit.

"Don't worry, I'll like anything you do."

I dropped to my knees, thought back on what my call girl BFF shared, then licked the head like a lollipop.

24

THEO

I PRIDED myself on being in control. Being focused and clear headed in all situations. But when Mallory finished licking every inch of my dick with her little pink tongue then took the head into her mouth, I lost it.

The woman... she, *fuck.*

Holy shit.

"Mal–"

Then her tongue shifted back and forth on the sensitive spot at the back of the corona and my hips bucked involuntarily.

"Holy shit, what the–"

She started to take me deeper, then deeper still.

I groaned. When I first met Mallory over the summer, I'd been instantly hot for her. Imagined her sucking my dick. What guy didn't imagine a hot woman blowing him? Things had been cold with Maude for a long time–had they ever not been?–but meeting Mallory changed things somehow.

I was pretty fucking happy when I found Maude with someone else. Now I knew why. Because Maude was not the woman for me. I needed heat. Passion. Sass and feistiness. And a woman who was blowing my fucking mind.

Mallory pulled back slightly, as if surprised by having something so big filling her mouth, then with a determined look, took even more of me. More than I ever expected. More than... holy hell.

"Fuck!" I shouted. The noise bounced off the walls of the small living room. I set my hand on her head, tangling my fingers in her silky hair. Oh shit, she was destroying me. This was–

She hummed–hummed!–as her hands cupped my ass to hold me in place, the vibrations a sweet torture. Then I watched as my dick disappeared. Slowly. Really fucking slowly so her hot, wet heat surrounded more and more of me.

She had to stop. She was going to stop. She couldn't take more. She–

She took it all.

"Holy fuck." I bumped the back of her throat and saw God.

With another little hum, she pulled back slightly, then looked up at me.

Looked. Up.

"You've... you've never done this before?"

The *mmmhmm* sound she made was a no and the vibrations tightened my balls.

Mallory was on her knees, her lips stretched around my dick, and she met my gaze, breathing deeply through her nose. Then her eyes narrowed as if challenged or dared before looking down.

In, out she went, literally fucking me with her mouth, all the while holding me in place.

"Shit, you don't have a gag reflex." My voice tumbled out of me, and my legs went weak as her flattened tongue slid along the underside. I stroked her hair, then she pulled off. Her lips were slick and swollen, her cheeks flushed, her gaze eager to please and so fucking earnest.

I thought she might be done, taking me like a good girl for her first time but getting tired. But she swallowed hard, licked her lips, then put two fingers into her mouth. Sucked.

Enthralled like a teenager seeing his first porno, I watched her pull them out and showed me they were slick. Then she took me deep again, practically throat fucking herself. Wet, slurpy sounds filled the room as she literally fucked me with her mouth.

I could barely catch my breath it was so intense. "Fuck, Mal. I'm–"

I was going to come. My balls drew up, the tingling at the base of my spine the indication I wasn't going to last much longer. Which hadn't been very long at all. A minute, even?

Her hands pushed down the back of my jeans and boxers so they rested even lower on my hips.

"Pull off so I–"

I was going to say *so I don't come down your throat,* but

she did some licking, swirling thing with her tongue while taking me deeper yet.

Then fucking swallowing so the head of my dick was massaged by the ripples of her throat working. I'd never felt that before, the tight, hot vise.

Then–

"HOLY FUCK!"

She brushed one of those slick fingers against my asshole, then pressed into it.

I came involuntarily, instantly and so intensely I went blind.

25

MALLORY

I WIPED MY LIPS, which were curved up in a smile, diabolically thrilled and aroused at the same time about what just happened. Theo was sprawled on the couch where he'd pretty much tipped over like a tree chopped down in a forest, recovering.

Dazed.

Delirious.

Completely non-functioning.

The blow job had pretty much destroyed him.

Me and my mouth had conquered.

Ha!

His pants and boxers were still low on his hips. His dick was out, slick with spit and still hard. An intense orgasm like that and I thought a guy went soft. Not Theo.

I also didn't expect him to practically go unconscious either.

I mentally patted myself on the back for my newfound talent. I had Trixie and Annie to thank, that was for sure.

"Holy fuck," Theo said, tipping his head to the side, eyeing me. His cheeks were still flushed, and his dark gaze was still blurry. "What the hell was that?"

I frowned, suddenly unsure. "Um... a blow job."

"I thought you never did that before." His voice was ragged, and he was still trying to catch his breath.

"First time," I admitted. It was the truth, but clearly not every almost-virgin got tips from professionals. "Was it all right?"

Now I started to question myself. Maybe I'd messed up. Maybe it was always like that, or not as good as normal? It had been weird at first. A dick in your mouth? Odd. But then when Theo started responding, I thought I was doing okay. Then, I followed every one of Annie's and Trixie's late-night tips, the tongue flick, the swirl, even the back door one. I'd questioned that one, but Annie had assured me a guy would blast off like a rocket from it and... Theo had.

It had been weird to breathe through my nose, then not at all when he'd been so deep, but hearing him shout like that? The way it felt having him swell, then throb against my tongue? Powerful. Exhilarating.

His gaze narrowed. "You take a class with bananas or something?"

I shrugged, stood. There was no way in hell I was telling him I learned blow job techniques in the Las Vegas Detention Center from professional call girls. "Just because I've never done something before doesn't mean I'm not any good at it."

My knees were a little sore. I wondered if Trixie or Annie used knee pads.

"You don't have a gag reflex."

"Don't go all doctor on me now," I said. I'd had no idea until now that I didn't have gagging issues.

He stared up at me, still not moving.

"Doctor?" he asked. "Hell, woman. I don't even remember my name let alone my profession after an experience like that."

He wasn't so serious now. Or uptight. I'd never seen him so relaxed. Or stunned.

"I'm glad you liked it," I said primly, but inwardly thrilled.

He reached out, took my hand, then tugged me down on top of him.

I let out an oomph and set my hands on his chest. I could feel him, hard beneath my belly.

He stroked my hair back, studied me like I was a newly found creature in the rainforest. "Liked it? I may have died there for a minute."

I grinned. He grinned back. Cupping the back of my neck, he gently pulled me down for a kiss.

Our first kiss.

26

THEO

"–TONGUE DEPRESSORS. ANYTHING ELSE?"

I blinked, then realized Verna had been talking to me. She even asked me a question. "Huh?"

I was leaning against the front desk, and I pushed off because I was slumping like a teenager.

She smiled. "Where did you just go, and can I join you on that trip?"

I wasn't thinking about work. Or listening. It had been over twelve hours and I was *still* thinking about that blow job.

Holy fuck.

"Sorry, didn't sleep great." Grabbing the business cards from the little stand, I fiddled with them, then stuck them back.

That was a complete and total lie. I slept like a fucking

baby. That was what having the cum sucked from your balls did to a guy.

"Mmmhmm," she said, eyeing me skeptically. One week in and she knew my signs.

"You only had one cup of coffee, you didn't mind handling the three-year-old with hives or Mrs. Krase and her incessant chatter."

"Kids aren't that bad, and Mrs. Krase is lonely and only wants to visit."

Her mouth dropped open a bit, watching me as I moved the laminated school calendar, used to schedule appointments around kids' days off, to the right a few inches.

"Kids aren't bad?" she asked with a stunned look. "You know why Mrs. Krase keeps coming in?"

I shrugged. "I don't want any kids of my own, but it seems they just want to have fun all the time. And not itch. What's wrong with that? The same probably goes for Mrs. Krase as well. The fun part. Well, probably the itching, too."

She blinked. "You're probably right," she said warily, wondering if I'd been possessed by not a demon, but maybe the tooth fairy or something else bright and sparkly. The phone rang and she turned to answer it but spun back. "Oh, Mac called. He said you're having lunch with him and the daytime crew. Noon. Your leftover beef stew can hold until tomorrow and I gave Jeff your one o'clock so you don't have to rush back."

I left her to tackle the call since she seemed to be organizing not only my work schedule but what I ate for lunch and who I ate it with.

Verna was a boss bitch.

The other boss? Mac. I wondered what he had in store for me today. Burning building rescue? Trapped in an air duct? All a part of small town life. It was like that satellite channel my mother always talked about, with the small town a big city doctor returned to and fell in love. Small town life wasn't that bad. Kids? Not horrible. People? I could tolerate them conscious. Especially Mallory. And her hot, talented, ruthless mouth. I wouldn't call a blow job romantic, but I sure as hell would be up for another.

She and I kissed for a while after that out of body experience. On the mouth. Just kissing as I got my brain cells back. Or regrew new synapses since mine had been blown along with my dick.

There had been no reciprocation, me getting my mouth back on Mallory's perfect pussy and making her scream my name and every swear word she refused to say, because I'd gotten a call from Jeff. I'd answered because I thought it might have been about a patient–and I'd had a decade of responding to pages and calls, every one of them critical–but it was a last-minute invitation to dinner. I wanted to say no, but Verna would have wanted a legit reason for turning the offer down. Fooling around with Mallory wouldn't cut it and I didn't want to explain what the two of us were up to. Even I didn't know.

With my brain fried, I hadn't been able to think of anything but saying yes. So Mallory and her pussy were traded for double servings of Verna's infamous beef stew. It had been delicious, but not what I'd wanted to put in my mouth.

Sticking her head in the office, London said, "Patient in room two is ready."

"Thanks."

I pulled out my phone and sent Mallory a quick text.

My place again. Six. This time I get to eat.

I didn't expect her to reply since she was working, so I left my cell on my desk. As I slung my stethoscope around my neck, I envisioned her surrounded by kids in short little chairs singing songs or coloring pictures. A completely different–and far more innocent–mental picture than the one from last night of her on her knees, my cock buried in her throat and her finger in my–

Now I was hard. Fuck!

MALLORY

"I NEED SOME SHIFTS," I said to my brother.

School ended at two-thirty, so I was usually done with paperwork and prepping for the next day an hour after that. That made it between busy times of lunch and dinner when I went into my brother's bar.

I found him in the back storeroom, counting liquor bottles, clipboard and pen in hand.

He turned at my voice and offered me a smile, then wrote something down on the inventory sheet. "Hey. How come?"

I'd asked before, especially during college, to grab some extra cash on breaks or long weekends. I always had a job of my own, but often wanted a little extra and he made it easy for a quick shift pickup here and there.

"Saving up for the house."

It was the truth. I *was* saving for Mrs. Jonsdottir's place, but for now it was being redirected to Las Vegas. No way in hell was Arlo learning what happened. We didn't talk about our sex lives. His actual one and my non-existent one. Well, budding one since I'd done some obscenely hot things with Theo.

Things he wanted to do again since he'd texted me for another six o'clock get together.

I'd rocked his world with a blow job. No question. It had been strange at first, having something so big in my mouth. It was Theo's responses, the sounds, tensing of muscles, tugging my hair, that spurred me on. I might have been using my hooker friends' tips as my only guide on what to do, but I'd felt powerful.

But he'd been called out and I'd gone home, the exchange over.

Maybe I was mixing sexy times with interest or growing feelings, but I liked Theo. Not just found his photo hot on his brother's computer and made empty statements about marrying him when we'd never even met, but actual liking.

He was... nice. It was clear when he was with his brothers that they had a great bond. He was kind; no one fed a stray cat if he didn't have a generous and concerned nature. He was devoted. He spent close to fifteen years of his life training to be a doctor to save people. Which he did.

He was also ridiculously introverted. Quiet. Closed off. Focused. Even a little... distant. Even when we were getting each other off, it wasn't intimate.

I had to be cautious with him. I could fall hard, and he'd shrug and move on to his laundry or write a medical journal article or something. Also, I didn't want to get too close because he'd see the real me. The one that hid behind her bold words and loud ways. Who knew she wasn't lovable enough to keep, or to love unconditionally. There were rules attached with loving me. Boundaries. Expectations.

I was good to fuck. I knew that. Theo saw me as a task. A mission to get the almost-virgin some experience and orgasms. He'd be clinical and get me off and get his own pleasure, but nothing more.

That was fine.

Fine!

Why? Because I never stopped thinking about him licking my pussy. Or the way his fingers worked me to orgasm in record time. Or the few kisses we'd shared that had made me feel more than I should.

"Mal?" Arlo asked. "How come you need some shifts?"

I startled, realized I'd spaced out, thinking about Theo.

I couldn't tell Arlo the truth. We might be close, but no guy wanted to find out his sister was arrested for being a hooker.

There was a line. Had to be.

"If money's tight, you can move in with me," he offered, although I knew he wasn't serious.

I glanced up at the ceiling, as if I could see through it to his small apartment above the bar. "I'm too old to couch surf because that's all I'd get."

His place was a small one bedroom. He could probably afford something bigger and not live over his work, but he was a bachelor and worked a lot. He was content.

He put down the clipboard and tucked the pen behind his ear. We looked a lot alike. Same hair, although his was cut in the trendy style with the sides shorn close and the top longer. His blue eyes held more mischief than sass.

"Wait. Your mom's not bothering you again, is she?"

"Cheryl?"

Arlo and I shared the same dad, but we had different moms. His died when he was young and a few years later, his dad started getting out there and fell for Cheryl. They married because she was a gold digger and thought our dad would be a sugar daddy for her. Except the money he'd had was from his dead wife–Arlo's mom–and he drank his way through it, but only after my mother got pregnant with me.

Since she didn't like to work, she stuck around. Except neither of them really wanted to work. Dad lost himself in the bottom of a beer keg and was content with his consistent but dead-end job. Cheryl hadn't been happy with any of it, and sank into a life of... entitlement, without any money to go with it.

Arlo was eight years older than me, enough where he was really protective, but also hadn't been around much after I turned ten. The day after graduation, he'd moved out. I didn't blame him. I did the same thing.

Except Cheryl wasn't his and he'd never liked her. She knew it, too. There was no love lost there. That was why she never asked him for money like she did me. Or let me forget the burden I was to her.

I didn't answer his question, only looked away.

He groaned. "What now?"

Instead of telling him, I pulled my phone from my purse, found the text she'd sent during the school day.

> The car needed more work. I told the repair
> shop you'd be in to pay the bill by Friday.

He swore under his breath. "Don't pay it."

"I can't," I admitted.

He studied me, understanding what I meant. I didn't have money for her, or me. With a nod, he said, "If I give you shifts, you better not give her any of the tips. No way are you fucking working your ass off for her."

I shook my head. I felt the guilt always associated with Cheryl, but she was bumped down on my worry list because of everything else in my life.

He scratched his head, which I knew was a gesture to keep his hand busy instead of strangling me. "What did you give her this month?"

I gnawed on my lip, knowing he wasn't going to like the answer. "Rent."

He exhaled, closed his eyes. "Fuck, Mal. She's never going to stop."

"Am I supposed to just cut her off?"

"Yes!" he huffed.

This was the same argument we got into again and again.

He came over, set his hands on my shoulders. "You will never make her happy."

I looked down and sniffed. That hurt. The words and the truth behind them.

"Fuck, I don't mean it like that." He sighed, softened his voice. "You're perfect. She's a fucking mooch and no matter what you do, she will never be satisfied. A new car, she'll say she expected four-wheel drive. A new coffee maker and it should have been an espresso machine."

He looked down at the phone, swiped back through the older texts she sent.

"You paid the electric bill last month? Fuck, Mal, look at this text! She's gaslighting you when you got upset about giving her a hundred bucks."

"I know. I know! But she–"

He held up his hand. "No buts. You can't give her money you don't have. You work your butt off and should be tucked away in that little dream house of yours. I'm so fucking proud of you."

Tears filled my eyes because Arlo was more a parent than either of mine.

"But you've been giving her money for *her* rent and other shit and then knocking that you're only a teacher and don't make more. Like it's your fault she's a deadbeat."

She said it was, that I was the baby she never wanted. That she wouldn't be working a long line of deadend jobs if she hadn't had me. I tried for her to love me. Tried all the time growing up. In college. Now. No matter what I did, it wasn't good enough because *I* wasn't good enough.

"She has to take care of Dad," I offered, although the excuse was lame.

"Really? You're going with that? You're too fucking nice, Mal. Dad is a doormat, and you know it. He lost himself in a bottle when my mom died. The house could blow away in a tornado and he'd be content as long as he has his beer, cigs, and his recliner."

That was completely true.

"You know I don't trust her. Hell, I wonder why she even stays."

I wondered, too. If she never wanted me, if Dad never turned into the money catch she'd hoped for, it was a mystery why she stuck around.

He shook his head. "She takes advantage. I have to wonder what she's really up to these days. If you paid her rent and fucking electric bill, how come she doesn't have money for the car? Is she really working even?"

I had no answer.

"Maybe it's time to find out."

I recognized that look, the determined gleam I often saw in my own. Not now, and never with Cheryl.

"Go for it," I told him. "All I know is I want some shifts."

When he eyed me like big brothers do as if trying to figure out if he was being fucked with, I added, "For the house."

He must have believed me. "You can come to me for money, you know."

I held up my hand. "We just had a huge talk about Cheryl mooching for money. I will not turn into her."

He laughed. "Right. You could never be like her. Ever. You have a good heart."

I wasn't so sure, and I tried as hard as I could not to be. I worried, like an alcoholic with a bottle of whiskey, that once I started asking for money like she did, I wouldn't be able to stop.

First Bridge for my ticket home. What next?

I didn't take handouts. Not from Arlo.

"I'll earn the money, big brother. Giving me the shifts is generous enough."

He handed me my phone back. "Okay. Tonight will be too quiet to need you. Besides, don't you usually do yoga on Tuesdays?"

I nodded. I didn't go last week since Bridge and I ended up eating pizza next door instead.

"Work Friday and Saturday. They'll be busy and get you good tips."

I nodded, relieved. Relief made me smile. "Thanks, A."

Maybe I'd have the money to get to Vegas after all.

28

THEO

> Can't come at 6.

WHEN I READ Mallory's text, I immediately thought of some inappropriate comment about how she would be coming if she just stopped by. I'd ensure it. Before I could respond, she sent another text.

> Yoga. Join me.

Join her?

"What's the look about?" Verna asked.

My last patient of the day had just walked out the door. Jeff was still in with one, but then we'd be closing up. Verna was finalizing paperwork and making the last of the next day appointment reminder calls.

I looked up from my phone.

"Know anything about yoga?"

Her eyes widened. "That was not what I was expecting you to say."

I frowned, leaned on the high counter to meet her gaze. "Oh? What were you imagining?"

She thought about it. "Your IRA is maturing."

"My IRA is maturing?" I repeated. "You do know I'm a billionaire, right?"

I wasn't tossing that out there to be obnoxious, but Verna knew everything, which meant she knew I didn't need a retirement plan.

"Doesn't matter. That's what would come out of your mouth. That or... the folic acid in kale is too valuable to avoid because of the bitter taste."

"Kale?" I blinked at her. "Am I really that boring? That dull?"

"You said you're a billionaire."

"So? I'm not going to sit around and fan myself with hundred dollar bills all day."

"I appreciate that you and your brothers are all valuable members of society. That you want to help in emergencies is gallant."

"Gallant. What am I, King Arthur?"

She pursed her lips at my sass.

"Why did you quit the hospital in Denver?"

She eyed me. I eyed her right back.

"I realized I was turning into something I didn't like."

"Turning, or already were?" she asked. Her voice was softer now, as if the change in our conversation was hitting a more personal vibe.

"What are you getting at?"

"Your cases may have been unique, but your life was monotonous. Boring."

"Thanks, Verna," I replied, suddenly grouchy. Not because she wasn't being nice, but because she was truthful. I couldn't remember when I wasn't boring.

She gave me a sad smile, which I didn't like in the least. "You moved to live life. So do it."

"That why Jeff made me do that fire training on Saturday?"

Her mouth turned up. "I knew you'd become friends with Mac."

"This isn't kindergarten and meeting a kid on the playground."

"For you it is. You're in the kindergarten of your life. Go have some fun. Go do yoga."

"Why did we have this entire conversation? I started with yoga."

She shrugged. "You asked me if I know anything about yoga."

"Right. So, do you?"

"All I know is it's going to be fun for anyone watching you try it out."

"Why's that?"

"It's harder than it looks, for one. And the ladies are going to enjoy ogling your butt in downward dog."

I frowned because I had no idea what downward dog was. I pushed off the counter and walked off, her laughter following behind me. "Me and my IRA are out of here," I called. "Have a good night."

29

MALLORY

"You came," I said, staring at Theo in surprise.

He showed up to yoga. In workout shorts and a snug t-shirt. Even though I'd had his dick in my mouth, I'd never seen him in anything but jeans or khakis and a button up. Even over the summer, I didn't remember him wearing anything else.

And I remembered everything about Theo.

He nodded, although he looked as if he'd been coerced, or perhaps dared, to be here.

"Hi there. Welcome to class," Aspen said, weaving her way between the rolled out mats of the others in the class to introduce herself.

"Theo, this is Aspen. This is her studio. This is Theo James, Mav's brother."

Aspen was open and generous and calm where I was loud and obnoxious. Her energy was soothing and mine seemed... snarled. She was so flipping chill and pretty I hated her sometimes.

"Great place," he said, glancing around. The studio was on the second floor of an old building on Main Street. The ceilings were tall, the walls plain brick. Soft music came from speakers in the corners. Hints of lavender and citrus were in the air.

She shook Theo's hand. "First time?"

There was no innuendo there, but it made me blush since the basis for our entire relationship–me and Theo– was based on sex.

"Yes. I'm trying new things," he replied.

I realized how attractive a couple they'd make. Aspen, tall and willowy and relaxed all the time beside Theo's handsome good looks and intelligence. She'd soothe his hard edges and he'd not rile her up or mess with her chakras or anything.

But he didn't offer her more than a neutral smile and his gaze didn't drop to her sports bar and snug leggings.

"I'll get you a mat and some blocks."

When she left to do that, Theo leaned in. "Will you be gentle with me?" His question was *all* innuendo.

I rolled my eyes. "You don't want gentle."

Aspen came our way and he offered her a glance, but replied to me. "No, I don't want gentle."

"Here you go." She handed him a rolled mat and set two blocks on the glossy wood floor. "Any injuries or anything I need to be aware of?"

"He's a doctor," I told her.

Her eyes widened in awareness. "You're Dr. Robinson's replacement."

Theo nodded. "That's me."

"Welcome to Hunter Valley. Follow anyone in the class if you get lost, but you can't go wrong with keeping your eyes on Mallory."

She winked at me.

I flushed.

"I will," he replied.

"Two rules in my class," Aspen offered. "If it hurts, stop doing it. And most of all, have fun."

"Fun. Right."

30

THEO

HAVE FUN.

Have fun.

Why was everyone telling me to have fun?

Fun sucked.

Yoga was fun? Holy fuck, yoga was hell. Bending and reaching and holding poses and breathing and... FUCK.

"Breathe in, forward fold. Breathe out, halfway lift. Breathe in, forward fold. Breathe out, step back, plank."

Aspen's melodic–and evil–voice cued our moves. Since I had no idea what most of what she said meant, I kept one eye on Mallory. And because watching her bend and move was hot as fuck. But I was too miserable to appreciate how flexible she was.

Plank I could do. I held myself at the top of a push up.

"Go through your flow and meet in downward dog."

I lost count of how many times she said that, and I still

didn't have it. Watching Mallory again, I lowered myself into a low pushup, then up in a weird stretchy sphinx pose, then shifted back, ass up and into downward dog.

From the thirty other times or so we'd been in this position, I knew Aspen would hold us here for at least a few seconds. I took those few moments to turn my head and gaze, upside down, at Mallory, only to discover she was looking at me.

And smiling. Grinning, really. Then she gave me that same funny face when I'd told the first graders at the assembly about communicable diseases.

I couldn't help but grin back.

"Doing okay?" she asked.

"This is fucking hard," I replied, shifting my palms on the mat.

"It's fun," she replied. Her long hair was up in a sloppy bun on top of her head and her cheeks were flushed from exertion.

I was sweating like a pig.

"Is it extra hot in here?"

"Yeah, it's not quite hot yoga, but the heat's turned up."

Who the hell turned the heat *up* for a workout? "Why?"

"To make you sweat," she said, but probably wanted to add on *Duh.*

"Right leg up and back," Aspen cued.

Mallory stuck her right leg up and out behind her. I followed.

"Bring it up, curl knee to nose."

I brought my knee up underneath me but there was no way in hell it was getting anywhere near my nose. I wasn't that flexible, and I felt my core quiver at the attempt. I grunted and Mallory laughed.

I got frustrated and growled.

Mallory kept right on laughing.

"Plant your foot, Warrior Two."

I looked to Mallory and followed. She came up into a stance with her front leg bent, back leg straight out behind, arms up and out at shoulder height, moving almost effortlessly.

I was lightheaded and sweat dripped down my temples. I grabbed the hem of my t-shirt and wiped my face.

"Peaceful Warrior."

Mallory leaned back, stuck her right arm straight up.

I grunted at the flex in my back when I mimicked her.

"Extended side angle."

Mallory dropped her arm and leaned forward, rested her elbow on her right knee.

I copied her again. "You do this all the time?" I murmured.

Mallory grinned. "I love it. Theo, you look miserable."

"This isn't fun," I said, my right thigh burning from holding the pose.

"There's no winning in yoga," she said. "You don't have to do anything perfect."

Said the woman holding a perfect pose and glistening with sweat, not melting like a snowman in July like I was.

"That's right, Mallory," Aspen said, picking up on Mallory's words. "You're here, you showed up for class. That's yoga. If you can't smile while doing yoga, when can you smile?"

I gave the woman–who seemed so quiet and placid but was actually a ruthless taskmaster–a doubtful look.

"Life's not easy. Shit happens," she added.

The others in the class hooted and called out their agreement from their extended side angle misery.

My mind immediately went to all the trauma patients I had over the years, which was pretty much a daily occurrence, then to the last one, the boy who'd died in surgery. Shit definitely happened, and when it did, I was supposed to feel something. Anger, sadness.

"This is easy," Aspen pushed on. "Simple. Just be. There's no competition, no winning. Just be."

"Just be," I muttered. "Have fun."

"Yes, let's have some fun," Aspen added, seemingly taking my words to heart. "Time for Bird of Paradise pose."

Everyone started to laugh and groan, which meant I wasn't going to like it.

On her mat in the front of the class, Aspen moved into the pose we were all holding, then added on. I listened and watched her with growing horror.

"Bind your hands, bring your right foot back to your left, then slowly lift, lift, lift, then foot to the sky."

"Holy fuck," I whispered, rising up out of the pose and stared at Aspen in disbelief. She was standing on one foot, her arm wrapped around her back and the other around her leg that was raised in the air and pointed toward the sky. She looked like she was in *Cirque du Soleil* or some other contortionist show. Or a Bird of Paradise flower.

I looked on as everyone in the class started to work on the pose to varying degrees of success, talking and laughing as they tried. One woman got her hands bound, one arm behind the back, the other through the legs to have the hands clasped together. One got her feet together but that was it. She looked... tangled bent over like she was. Another was slowly lifting her leg, balancing precariously.

Then there was Mallory, who got her leg up just like Aspen, then stumbled and fell out of the pose. She laughed, then tried again. This time, she failed at bringing her legs together, stumbled, then stood and laughed some more.

I couldn't help but smile at her efforts, the way she tried, failed, and just... had fun.

I shook my head, amused.

She turned to me, eyes rolling. "You try."

I held up my hand. "Hell no."

"Just the bind."

Just the bind. As if that didn't look hard enough.

I gave her a look, but she gave me a look back.

"Fuck," I muttered before shifting into the initial pose, but couldn't figure out how my arms went from there. Mallory took my left arm and bent it behind my back as she helped move my right to reach beneath my thigh and then behind.

"Good!" she praised as I struggled to reach the tips of my fingers together, then curled in and clung. Barely.

My breathing was ragged from exertion, the sweat falling non-stop.

"Now bring your legs together," she added. The soft feel of her hand on my hip had me attempting. I felt like I'd been hogtied while trying to stand upright at the same time. An inch, then another. Then–I lost my balance and tipped, but I let go of my hold and stopped my fall.

I stood, caught my breath and found myself... smiling.

Everyone clapped for me, and Aspen came over and squeezed my arm. I felt my cheeks heat with embarrassment.

Mallory gave me a spontaneous hug, then pulled back, laughing. "See? Fun!"

I shook my head at her glee. At the class's praise at my sad efforts.

I'd failed, all my faults and weaknesses on display, but nothing happened. No one yelled. No one shamed me. No one died.

I'd been applauded and... hugged because it was just yoga.

As Aspen settled everyone down onto their mats for the winding down of class, which, from what I could tell, was to lie on your back and take a nap, I realized I took shit way too seriously. I just tried to turn myself into a fucking pretzel and was pissed that I failed. Of course I failed. I never imagined even trying. Ever.

But I did, at Mallory's prodding. And I'd felt serious, then ridiculously silly, then... amused.

Once settled on my mat, eyes closed, Mallory's hand found mine and held it. And didn't let go.

31

MALLORY

WE ENDED up at the pizza place after class, having put in our order with Otis when we came in and seated at a two-top in the corner. Now we were arguing.

"I'm not going back," he said, taking a hearty gulp from his water glass.

"Why not? You did great."

He leaned forward. "I did it with the hopes of getting in your pants."

My mouth fell open in surprise. He wasn't shy or reserved in his sexuality. I just hadn't expected him to admit it outright in a restaurant.

"Seeing you in those snug clothes was a perk."

I narrowed my eyes at his look. The look that said he wasn't lying. That he was hungry, and for more than just pizza.

"You've got a pretty fine ass yourself," I said, turning it

back around on him. "And other parts." I licked my lips and he got my drift.

His gaze was heated, and now his face was hot.

This banter wasn't working. I was getting turned on. I wasn't experienced with it. The last time I did it, I got arrested. It was one thing to sling innuendos around when they meant nothing, which was what I thought was the case in Las Vegas.

It was another when it was with a guy–the only guy–to give me orgasms. And good ones. It was as if the seal had been broken on my need for sex. Now that I knew what it was like, at least almost-sex, I was insatiable.

"Theo," I whispered.

"After we have our pizza," he said, picking up on my need. His dark gaze dropped to my lips. "Then I'll eat you."

I tried to stifle a whimper, but he heard it. The corner of his mouth tipped up.

"Here it is," Otis said, setting a small pizza on the table between us, forcing us to lean back in our seats. "Going to introduce me to your friend, Mal?"

Otis hovered over our table, waiting.

"Otis, this is Theo James. He's Mav's brother." Otis had met Mav a bunch since he and Bridge frequently ordered carry out.

"Theo, meet Otis. This is his place."

They shook hands and Otis eyed him, then me, then him, then me again.

Otis leaned toward me and whispered, "This guy know about your talented vagina?"

I gasped, completely and totally appalled. He remembered what Bridge and I asked him the week before about whether he was looking for a talented vagina when sleeping with a woman. The little shit turned it around on me. The grin on his face, and the wink, screamed *payback*.

With a quick glance at Theo, I knew he heard. His jaw clenched and the way he looked at Otis I worried he was going to do him harm and not treat him for his injuries after.

"What did you just say to her?" Theo asked, his voice low and... yeah, deadly. He pushed his chair back as if ready for a confrontation.

I stood, pushed Otis back a few steps, making him laugh. "You're an idiot," I told him, just like usual with my brother or one of his friends. "It's a joke. An inside joke," I added for Theo's benefit.

Otis laughed and I blushed furiously. I pushed him again. He was big and would've stood up to me if he really wanted, but he'd had his fun. "Go away, you moron."

He walked off, smartly behind the counter where it was probably safer.

Before I could sit, Theo tugged me down onto his lap. I had no choice but to look at him. We weren't the only ones eating. A few tables were occupied with others having a casual dinner.

"Did you sleep with him?" he asked, his voice a whisper and right in my ear. His warm breath fanned my neck and I shivered.

His voice was deep. His body tense. I swallowed hard.

"With Otis?" I cringed. "Um... no. He's one of my brother's friends. I've known him forever and that's just weird."

"Then why did he call your vagina talented?" he murmured.

I glanced around, but no one was paying us any attention. I squirmed on his lap because I realized... he was jealous. And that made me hot.

Leaning in close, I whispered right back, "You had your fingers in me. Besides being wet, did you find it... talented?"

I felt a growl reverberate through his chest more than hear it.

"You said if I wanted to have sex, it would be with you," I said. Against my hip, I felt how hard he was. My pussy clenched, wanting that inside me. And not my mouth.

"That's right."

I set my palm on his jaw, felt the softness of his short beard. "I had my appointment yesterday. Got the shot. I'm covered."

Theo stood abruptly, set me on my feet. Pulling out his wallet, he tossed money on the table and dragged me out the door like a caveman, but not before I heard Otis call, "Have fun, kids!"

Have fun? With a possessive, eager Theo? Yes, please.

32

THEO

I'D NEVER MET anyone who tested my patience like Mallory. I understood now, perhaps, why people got hooked on drugs. The euphoria, the pure bliss of being lost in something, was addictive.

She, and that ridiculously talented vagina of hers, was addictive.

I knew what she felt like when she came.

I knew what she tasted like.

I knew what she looked like.

But I hadn't gotten inside her, and that was going to be dangerous. Because if my dick craved her without even being surrounded by her tight, wet heat, I wasn't sure if I could handle fucking her.

I was willing to take the risk.

We made it as far as slamming the front door behind us before I had my mouth on her. Thank fuck the pizza place was only around the corner. Any further and I'd have bent her over the nearest parked car.

My tongue was in her mouth, my hands in her hair and cupping her ass, she practically climbed my body. Fuck, she was a good kisser.

"Theo, please."

She was as desperate as me. But I was the one who knew what the hell was going to happen. Sure, her sixteen-year-old boyfriend's two thrusts gave her an idea, but this experience was going to be vastly different.

"What do you want?" I asked.

"You," she said, kissing along my jaw while tugging up the hem of my sweatshirt.

"You've got me."

"I want your dick."

"You can put it down your throat anytime you want."

Fuck, that had been insane. My balls were heavy and ached with that possibility again.

"No, you need to fuck me. Right now."

I spun her about, pressed her into the door. Rolled my hips. I wanted to take her to bed, to at least give her something soft at her back, but that wasn't going to happen now. Not this time.

Not with her frantic hands giving up on my sweatshirt and reaching into my workout shorts and taking hold of me.

"Fuck," I said, thrusting into her tight hold. I couldn't help the little laugh that escaped. Her eagerness was an insane turn on and I didn't want to come from a handjob. "Okay, okay."

I stepped back and her hand slipped away. Pulling out my wallet, I grabbed the condom I put there, just in case. I wasn't a Boy Scout, but it seemed my dick was always prepared.

Holding it up, I let her see it, to know what it implied.

She didn't respond, only frantically toed off her sneakers as she worked her tight yoga pants down her hips. I didn't know if she had panties on underneath because if she did, they fell to her ankles, too.

Before I could get the condom wrapper open, she toed the stretchy pants off one foot.

"Hurry," she breathed. She was bare for me from the waist down.

"Take off your top," I requested.

She shook her head, snagged the condom from my hold and pushed my shorts down, just enough so my dick sprang free. "No time."

With very sure hands, she rolled the condom down my length and the feel of her fingers on me pushed me over the edge.

Mallory. Bare pussy. Condom covered dick.

It was time.

I stepped into her again, hooked a hand behind her knees and picked her up, pressed her into the door.

I stared into her pale eyes. "You sure?"

Her eyes were blurry with need. She was breathing harder than she had at yoga class. Her cheeks were flushed. She was sure, but I needed to hear her say it.

"Yes."

"You wet?" No way was I taking her if she wasn't ready. With one hand on her bare ass and using the door to hold her up, I reached between us, found her pussy. Found it soaked.

"Theo!" she cried and grabbed the back of my head, tugged my hair. "If you don't fuck me right now I'm going to–"

I didn't let her finish, just shifted my hips enough so my dick was at her entrance, then thrust up and tugged her down at the same time.

"Fuck!" I cried.

She moaned.

And clenched around me.

And pulled my hair.

She was so fucking tight. Her inner walls rippled around me, adjusting to being filled. She'd barely ever had a dick in her before and I was big. I was cramming her full and I hadn't prepared her.

I dropped my face into her neck, licked and sucked at her damp skin, trying to hold still, to let her adjust.

"Theo," she whispered, angling her head.

I pulled back, met her blue, blue eyes.

"Okay?"

She nodded.

"You took all of me."

She nodded again.

"Ready to get fucked?"

Her inner walls clenched, and she nodded a third time.

"Good. Now you're going to find out what it's really like."

I pulled back, then punched deep. With each thrust, I used her hips and pulled her down on me. I wasn't gentle. I couldn't be. Not when her heels were pressed into my ass, getting me to go deeper.

"Yes!" she cried, pressing her head into the door.

I wished I could see her perfect tits, bite and suck at those tips, but she was covered in several layers–sweatshirt, stretchy top and sports bra. I'd savor the rest of her body later, but right now, it was to get her off on a dick for the first time.

My dick.

There was no way I could reach her clit in this position. Our bodies were too tight together. But I could touch her somewhere else. And I did.

Her eyes opened and flared wide as I pressed my thumb gently against her back door. I continued to fuck up into her as we looked at each other.

"Like that?" I asked.

She didn't answer because she probably wasn't sure. So I moved my thumb, collected some of her wetness and coated that place that *no one* had touched before. Then pressed in ever so slightly. Like she had with me.

"Theo."

Just my name, nothing more, but I felt her little rosette clench. Her pussy squeeze.

I grinned. "That's it. I knew you'd be wild. Whatever you need, tiger, I'll give it to you."

My balls drew up and I could feel my orgasm creeping up on me. I was going to come. I wasn't sure if I could hold it off though. She was too responsive. Too wet. Too tight. Too fucking perfect.

She licked her lips. "Please," she begged.

"More?" I continued to circle her carefully, even though my thrusts were anything but.

"More."

"Roll your hips. Rub your little clit and while I play with this virgin hole."

"Oh God. Your dirty talk…"

A smile tugged at my mouth as I carefully worked the pad of my thumb into her ass, carefully stretching her open. If she wanted ass play, I'd give it to her, but with lube and a lot of prep. This was just a glimmer, a test, to see what got her hot. Or got her off.

Because that was exactly what happened. Her hips rolled with a need to come and nudged my slickened thumb into her a little deeper, while I never stopped fucking her with my dick. I felt the end of her with how deep she took me.

"Fuck!" she screamed as she came, squeezing my dick so hard it was difficult to get nice and deep. Her scream was so loud, I felt immense male satisfaction that I could please her so well.

Caveman? Neanderthal? Whatever. She was riding my dick and I was satisfying my woman.

Yeah, my woman.

Because when I came, my dick so deep in her that she'd feel me for days, I knew I was addicted.

When she was slumped in my hold, our breaths finally slowing down, I reached up, stroked her hair back, although only a few wild strands had come loose from her bun.

"First time was against the door. Now I fuck you in a bed."

33

MALLORY

"SOMEONE KEEPS TEXTING YOU," Theo commented when my cell chimed from the other room. Again.

I sat on the edge of his bed, reaching down and pulling on my leggings. I'd tangled them earlier, not caring what happened to them in my haste to get naked. We'd had sex two more times–two!–before Theo climbed out of bed and tugged on his boxers.

I knew that was my sign it was time to go. The fact that he said he'd drive me home couldn't have been any clearer that I wasn't welcome to linger. That this had been sex and nothing more. Really amazing, insane, unbelievable sex.

Like, why had I held off for so long kind of sex.

Except, I had a feeling it was sex with Theo that made it so hot.

And that I was probably ruined for all other men.

I'd gone from low to no expectations to now insanely high ones that were probably untoppable.

While we'd had sex three times total, the number of orgasms was way higher than that. I didn't know I was multi-orgasmic. Or that there were so many different ways to fuck. Pressed up against the door had been rough. Wild. Frantic. I'd wanted him in me so bad I hadn't thought it through. Hell, I hadn't thought about much of anything.

He hadn't been gentle, not that I'd wanted it, filling me completely and really, really fast with a shift of his hips. It didn't hurt, like in a take-my-virginity sort of way. That had happened and I had a vibrator for practice. But Theo's dick?

Huge.

And talented. And hit all kinds of spots inside I didn't know I had. It was doing it with Theo that made it so good. I wanted it to be him. To feel him inside me. For him to *take* me.

Then again in bed after he'd stripped me bare and pretty much worshiped every inch of me. It'd been good because I was doing all those things with him.

Skill aside, I wasn't sure if it would have been as good with Tom, the history teacher. He was attractive, but the chemistry, the only I'd ever felt for a man, was shared with Theo.

I didn't expect to spend the night or anything; this had been completely spontaneous. Hell, if I'd known I'd have gone from yoga to Theo's front door to his bed, I'd have worn a cuter sports bra. At a minimum.

Of course there hadn't been sexy lingerie or seduction. It had been... instant need.

One minute we were staring at each other across the small table at Otis's, the next Theo's all growly and possessive and slamming me up against his front door.

The need had been soothed. For now. Except there was more than need.

There was *want* too. I wanted Theo and I was afraid it was for more than just sex.

My phone chimed again from the other room, prompting me that I'd been daydreaming. Although the dull ache between my thighs would be a long-term, real reminder.

"My mother," I told him. I glanced at him over my shoulder, then stood, tugging my leggings up the rest of the way. I only had on my pants and sports bra at this point. The rest of my clothes were in a pile beside me on the unmade bed.

"That's nice that you're close," he said, pulling on a pair of jeans, sliding up the zipper. Clothed, unclothed, half-clothed, Theo was gorgeous.

"We're not."

He stopped in the process of putting on a shirt he just pulled from a dresser. Waited.

"She wants money," I explained. Cheryl's behavior was no secret, especially from Bridge. And probably Mav now, too.

"For..."

"For whatever it is this time." I had no idea what it could be now. Oh yeah, the car repair bill which I never paid.

"What was it last time?" he stuck his head through the

hole of his shirt, pulling it down over his torso. A torso I'd licked not twenty minutes earlier.

His hair was a tousled mess. Because of my fingers.

"Rent. Electricity bill. Groceries, although this is probably another car repair."

I stood and it was my turn to put my shirt on.

Before I pulled it on, I saw him eyeing my chest in my sports bra. Yeah, not remotely sexy.

"Is she okay? And your dad?"

"My dad is fine. I'm sure he's in his recliner watching some game show right now with his beer and cigarettes. My mother is not okay," I grumbled, tugging my shirt down. "I mean, relatively speaking. She doesn't need a doctor or anything. She's... well, Arlo calls her a moocher."

"Arlo's your brother?"

I nodded.

"Does she bother him for money?"

I snagged my sweatshirt and carried it into the other room. I found my shoes and socks by the front door.

"No. She's his stepmom, so I'm the child to pester."

"Do you want her to stop?"

I spun and looked at him, leaning against the bedroom doorway. He was earnest in his questions, but they reminded me of Arlo's same ones.

"Yes. I want her to stop telling me I have to do it because it's my fault her life is ruined."

He frowned. "How did you ruin her life?"

"By being born," I muttered, then dropped onto the edge of the sofa to put my shoes and socks on.

"Wait, wait. What?" He came over and squatted down

before me when I didn't answer, even forced my chin up with his fingers. "What do you mean?"

I sighed. "She reminds me all the time when she got pregnant with me, her chances of being a model were over."

"You weren't there when your parents had sex."

I gave him a weird look, kinda like the one I made right before I threw up, because gross.

"It was her fault," he added, but I didn't like thinking about being a *fault*.

My cell chimed again, and I rolled my eyes.

"Doesn't matter."

"My father didn't give a shit about me or my brothers," he admitted. "He was an asshole."

"You don't take his calls?" I asked.

"He's dead." The way he said it, with a flatness of someone who wasn't the least bit sad about it, revealed more about their father-son relationship than anything else. All four James brothers were good men. Nice. Kind. Gentlemen–at least Theo was until he... wasn't. I had to wonder what made the guy so hated.

"So no." I stood, forcing him to stand as well, or fall on his ass. "I'm sorry to hear about your father."

He shrugged, going to the front door and grabbing his keys from the little side table where he'd dropped them when we came in, all hot and heavy. "I'm not. Ask Mav. Our dad fucked younger women. Like just legal. That messed with Mav over Bridget."

I imagined.

"With Dex, it turns out the guy would drop him off at

hockey practice and go off and fuck some of the moms. Or snack bar workers."

I wrinkled my nose, thinking of an older guy skeeving on the college girls who worked at the winter complex.

"Silas? Not sure of his issues yet with the guy, but I'm sure they'll surface one of these days when we drink too much."

"And you?"

He shrugged. "My father was a narcissist, but he pretty much ignored me. I had it easy."

Thinking of Cheryl, I wondered if being ignored would be so much better. I'd know where I stood then. Nowhere in her life. "I can't just cut her off," I said, switching back to Cheryl.

"Why not? She's an adult." His own experiences skewed his perspective. He wouldn't understand because the situation wasn't anything like his had been.

"Because... because..." I said again, not wanting to say it aloud. She was the one person who was supposed to offer unconditional love. I barely remembered Bridge's parents before they died, but they'd been awesome. Then Lindy took over and pretty much raised me and Bridge together since my parents weren't the greatest. I just... always hoped I was worth more to Cheryl than just being a piggy bank.

He must have sensed I wasn't sharing more because he took my hand and pulled me in for a kiss.

A kiss!

I held on to his jacket as he took his time. This wasn't hurried and it felt more intimate than the sex we just had. As if he was trying to soothe me with his mouth.

It was working. I felt safe with him. Not only was he in

tune with me sexually, but he seemed aware of my needs, that I could seek comfort from him.

After some indeterminate time, he led me to his car. Kissing–and talking about our parents–was over. So was our time together.

Ten minutes later, I was well-sexed and opened my apartment door and saw my roommate and her boyfriend... getting well-sexed on the couch.

They came up for air and Maggie covered up her bare chest with one of the throw pillows.

"Mal! Hey!" She smiled and looked only a little embarrassed.

"Hi," I said, turning toward the kitchen and grabbing a drink from the fridge. I heard them moving around in the other room and a second later, she came into the kitchen.

"Guess what?" she asked, grinning.

"You had an orgasm?"

She laughed. "Well, we were getting there, but this!" She stuck out her hand and showed me a ring. "We're engaged!"

Nate, Maggie's boyfriend, came in, slung an arm around her shoulder. He was shirtless and grinning.

I couldn't help but smile at their happiness. A weird feeling came over me. Hot and sharp and oppressive, like jealousy and sadness. These two, fooling around and making out, loving each other, getting *engaged*. Then there was me, getting sex three times in a row and dropped off at home right after. Anyone would have thought that instead of getting naked and lots of big dick from Theo, we'd innocently watched Dex play hockey on TV.

The sex had been intense, but Theo and I shared nothing like what was so blatant between these two.

Love. Affection. A connection that was more than just chemistry.

"Congratulations! I'm so happy for you," I said. I was. Truly.

"Nate's living here now. He gave up his place in Havre and–"

I blinked and my stomach dropped. "What? Here?"

Our apartment was small. Two small bedrooms. One even smaller bathroom.

"I got transferred here," he explained, brushing his hair back from his face. He glanced at Maggie, then kissed the top of her head, as if he couldn't stop himself.

"Oh, wow. Um. Great."

"So, yeah, I think that you'll have to move out because we want to be on our own."

I knew that was coming next, but wow. Her words weren't cruel but fueled from a need to be alone with her new fiancé. The lease was in her name. I'd only taken over a sub-let and now renting a room to help her cover expenses until Mrs. Jonsdottir sold. I didn't have a legal standing here, although I didn't really want to linger living with her if they were going to be all hot and heavy all the time. Which they would be.

Mav and Bridge were. Gag. And I didn't have to live with them.

Nate nuzzled her neck and Maggie giggled. His hand slid down her back and gave her ass a squeeze.

"Right, I'll just be in my room."

I scooted past them and into my bedroom, closed the

door. Through the thin wood and walls, I couldn't miss how they got right back at it. I heard her bedroom door close, thank God, so there'd be two doors between their sexy times and me.

I pulled out my cell, read through Cheryl's texts which I'd ignored until now.

> You didn't pay the repair bill.

> Mallory, answer me.

> Don't be rude to your mother. Pay the bill before the manager of the service center calls you.

> Why are you so mean to me?

If I paid for the car repair, it would shut her up. Get her off my back. At least for a little while. And she'd stop saying I was mean. I sighed. I couldn't win because I *couldn't* pay the bill whether I was mean or not.

I hadn't had much time to think about a lawyer for my court date next week. I could get a public defender, but did they even believe I was innocent? Would he or she care about my fate one way or the other?

I didn't know lawyers in Las Vegas... but I knew two who might.

Maggie's headboard started to slam against the wall, breaking me from my thoughts.

Wham. Wham. Wham.

That and now she was crying out–and not in pain– probably a lot like I had earlier.

I dropped my head in my hands and groaned. I couldn't stay here, couldn't listen to them hump like rabbits.

I grabbed a bag, stuffed clothes for work into it along with my makeup kit and a few other things, then went to the only place I could think of. It wasn't Theo's. He made it obvious that while I was the woman he wanted to sleep with, I wasn't sleeping over. It wasn't Arlo's because I was too old for his couch and since he kept late hours with the bar, he'd wake me up, then I'd wake him up in the morning when I got up for school in turn. It sure as hell wasn't my parents. Mav and Bridge also fucked like rabbits, so there was only one place left.

Lindy's empty house. She'd moved to be with Dex in Denver, although she had no intention of selling the place. In fact, she and Dex had said they wanted to settle there after he retired in a few years.

For now, I was now a squatter.

34

THEO

WEDNESDAY, we fucked. It pretty much went like this: I texted for her to be at my house again at six. She arrived, went to the couch, pulled down her jeans and panties to just below her ass, then bent over the armrest. I'd almost come in my pants, but barely held off until I got her to come twice, my dick buried nice and deep. Oh, and my thumb in her ass. Then we'd gotten delivery from the Thai restaurant Mallory recommended, then, before she could put her chopsticks down, I manhandled her onto the floor and ate her out until she came. Twice. Yeah, I was a fucking caveman with the best dessert ever. Only then did I flip her over, pull her up on her knees and pull her hair as I took her from behind again.

Thursday. Yeah, Thursday. Sex was... adventurous. Holy fucking hell.

It was snowing and the roads were shit. I said I'd pick

her up. Not that she didn't drive in snow all winter long and she'd already been out in it going to work, but still. She'd resisted, but I told her the only way she'd sit on my lap and ride my dick–a position we hadn't done yet–was if I picked her up.

That was how I discovered she was staying at Lindy's house.

I brushed the snow off my head and coat when she let me in the front door. "Why are you staying here?" I asked.

She quickly shut the door behind me, cutting off the cold air.

She had on a black skirt with a flannel shirt and must've ditched her boots by the door because she only had tights that covered her legs and feet.

"Because my roommate got engaged and her boyfriend–fiancé–moved in with her and they're fucking like rabbits. I don't want to hear it."

I grinned, reached out and stroked her cheek. It clearly bothered her. I guess if I had a roommate ever, I'd be annoyed too. Probably jealous of them getting some and I wasn't. "We fuck like rabbits," I reminded.

"I thought rabbits had sex all the time. We only have it scheduled for six."

"Do you want it at another time?" I asked. I'd schedule it for whenever she wanted.

She raised a brow as if the question was odd.

"While she didn't kick me out on the street, I need to be out by the end of the month," she continued. "The sex spurred me to relocate quickly."

I looked around. Lindy's house–Bridge's too, technically, although she was permanently in Mav's place–was homey and warm. Nothing like any house I'd ever lived in. My parents' house had been a mansion. Massive. A showpiece. My apartment in Denver was where I slept and not much else since I'd pretty much lived at the hospital. Dex's apartment had been the same way. He was rarely there, traveling for hockey for most of the year. But Lindy was putting her stamp on the place now that it was hers as well. Mav's rental here was huge. And looked like a ski lodge. It wasn't their permanent house. I figured they would build something once the James Inn was complete. Silas' place wasn't all that much different.

We never had a home like this one as an example. The furniture was a random mix of old stuff from her parents' time and new pieces they must've picked up over the years. The kitchen appeared to have some brand-new appliances, probably a result of the tree falling on the house over the summer. It was lived in and comfortable.

"Nice place," I commented. "Cozy."

Mallory looked around, smiled at the place fondly. As if it were a person and she had intense feelings for it. "I pretty much grew up here. Lindy's pretty much my mom, but don't tell her that because she'll feel old. See that dent in the wall?"

I looked to where she pointed.

"I was mad when I didn't get the role of Sandy in the school musical *Grease* and I kicked the wall."

I knew the movie and imagined Mallory as Sandy. All sweet and innocent, but underneath, naughty as fuck. Yeah, that was her all right.

"Stay here then. I'm sure she won't mind."

She shook her head, moved into the family room. "No.

It's not mine. I'm okay crashing here, but I won't take advantage."

I frowned. "I'm sure Lindy and Bridget won't think that way."

"I'm getting a place of my own. The little house I told you about. It's going to be mine."

The gleam of determination in her eyes made me proud. It also made me want to see it happen. It sounded like she got the shaft from her mother–which I could relate–and needed a place to call her own. I wanted to help her. To make her life easier. To see her smile. There was something about Mallory I couldn't get enough of, and it wasn't just her pussy. Or her unbelievably talented mouth.

"I won't have to worry about roommates," she continued. "Or parents. Or listening to others having sex."

I approached her then, cupped her jaw, then slid my hand around to tangle my fingers in her ponytail. Then tugged. "Speaking of sex, I want you to ride me."

Her eyes widened and a flush swept prettily up her neck and cheeks. "Ride you?"

I nodded, took her hand and pulled her over to the couch. From my back pocket, I pulled out a condom I tucked in there before I left my place and dropped it onto one of the cushions. Then I went to work on the buttons of her shirt.

She licked her lips.

"That way you set the pace. And I can lick and suck on your pretty nipples."

A slow smile crept across her face. One thing about Mallory, she wasn't shy. When she liked something, she went for it. Like that blow job the other day. I'd been imagining her on my lap, cock buried deep all fucking day.

She reached for my jeans as I pushed her top off her shoulders. She let it fall to the floor as she got my zipper down, then jeans and boxers lowered. Barely. My dick sprang out as if eager and excited for her.

With a hand on my chest, she pushed and I dropped down on the couch. I couldn't help but laugh, then it ended quickly when she gave me the naughtiest, sexiest looks. Like me and my dick were at her mercy.

She reached under her skirt, worked the tights and–hopefully–her panties down and off. When she stood and moved to climb on my lap, I stopped her.

"Wait. Lift your skirt."

She frowned, not pleased to be stalled in her quest to ride my dick. But I needed to know she was ready. And I wanted a little show.

Grabbing the bottom of the flared material which fell to just above her knees, she raised it. Higher. Higher still until it was about her waist in the front and I could see her pussy.

"Wet?" I asked. "Need to make sure that pussy's ready for me."

She put her fingers between her thighs and swiped, and fuck me, raised her fingers to show me they were glistening. She was soaked.

"Get over here, woman," I growled.

She took a step closer, and I was able to hook a hand around her waist and pull her down. Once she was settled with her knees on either side of my hips, she put her sticky fingers to my lips and I sucked them clean. Now her taste was on my tongue and I was addicted. To her, to the fact that she was right here with me. Eager. *Ready.*

I reached for the condom and had that fucker on in record time.

"Up," I growled, and she went up on her knees. Grasping the base of my covered dick, I lined it up with her entrance. "Down."

And that was the last of me being in control. Because Mallory rode my dick with a wild abandon that made me lose my fucking mind.

She was rocking and bucking like a cowgirl on the back of a mustang. Her cries of pleasure, my name and every swear word she didn't want to say echoed off the family room walls. I wasn't all that quiet either. I told her she was a good girl. That she rode me so well. That her pussy was made just for my dick and only my dick. I may have even said take it, take all of it.

Until the doorbell rang, and she froze with my dick buried deep.

Turning our heads, we looked out the front window. There, at the curb, was a police car, blue emergency lights spinning on top, an officer at the door.

So as for Thursday's sex with Mallory? It was so good that the neighbor, Mr. VanMeyer, thought someone was being murdered.

Friday morning, I told Verna I was going to be a little late, went and bought Mallory a house and the old man next door some ear plugs.

35

MALLORY

"WHAT DO you mean you're crashing at a Vegas call girl's apartment?" Bridge asked. It was Saturday and I was at her and Mav's place for lunch. She'd pulled me into one of the downstairs bathrooms when I told her my plans around Tuesday's court appearance.

The guys–including Silas who'd flown up for the weekend–were out on the patio manning the grill. While it was a cold day–the snow had barely melted from the storm–Mav was cooking hamburgers. They'd shifted their dinner to lunchtime since I was working behind the bar for Arlo tonight. I'd made good tips the night before, enough to *hopefully* cover the lawyer's fee.

Even though the guys were outside, she'd dragged me to the other end of the house. It was great she was ensuring my secret stayed just that, a secret, but I was more inclined to think she was afraid we'd be interrupted.

"I'm crashing at a Vegas call girl's apartment," I confirmed.

She pushed her glasses up her nose and looked at me like I was crazy. Maybe I was, and not just for the sleepover with my new hooker friends. The night before, the police had cut off the very loud, very amazing sex with Theo. When she'd dragged me in here, at first I thought it was because she'd heard about that. But no. It was about my arrest and ensuing court date.

I had no idea who I was any longer. It was sex, sex, sex. Having sex, having sex loud enough for the cops to be called, being arrested for selling my body for sex. *Sex.*

Sex with Theo though, gah. I melted for him. Craved him. *Liked* him.

"What?"

"What do you mean, what?" she pushed.

"They're my friends." I thought of Annie and Trixie and how they'd kept me from freaking out being put in jail that night. It had been really flipping scary. Until they started chatting me up and gave me sexy times tips that had come in *very* handy.

"Are you serious?"

"Don't be judgy."

"I'm not *judgy*," she countered, absently straightening a hand towel. The powder room was as posh as the rest of the house, with a frosted window to let in tons of light and a heated toilet seat. "They're strangers."

"They're my friends," I repeated. "You forget I can make friends anywhere."

She huffed. "Like in lockup?"

"Exactly," I countered, a little hurt. She made it sound like I was a serial offender, where I hung out on a Saturday night to catch up just for fun. "Both women are really nice. I needed to find a local lawyer to represent me and they're the only people I know in the city to get a referral."

"Did they find you one?"

I nodded, then smiled. "Yeah, and she–the lawyer–said she'd represent me. Cheap."

Trixie had connected me with the woman, and we'd talked for a short time about my case. That it would be a quick ten minutes in court, and she was sure the charges would be dropped. She'd charge me only for the time before the judge, since she would already be at the courthouse for Trixie's and Annie's hearings.

Bridge eyed me warily. "Cheap like you're going to end up doing hard time because she's incompetent or cheap because she feels sorry for you?"

"Probably the latter." I thought for a moment because she was making me doubt myself, and the lawyer. "Hopefully not the first."

"Mal," she sighed.

"If Annie and Trixie haven't had any charges stick and they really *are* soliciting, then I feel confident she'll get me off." I did. I did. Aspen's manifesting in action.

She was quiet for a moment. "What's your plan then?"

"I'm driving down on Monday. Crash on Annie's couch that night. My court appearance is at nine-thirty on Tuesday morning. Then I'll drive back."

I checked and the flight cost so much more than it would to drive.

"You can use Mav's jet, I'm sure," she offered, sounding like someone becoming used to the *very* good things in life. Most people offered a shop vac or a ladder, not an airplane.

I wasn't looking forward to the thirteen hours on the highway... round trip, and I knew how nice the private jet was, but there was no way I could use it. I'd been ignoring Cheryl because I had no money to give her. I didn't want to hear her mean words or excuses, so I just didn't respond to her consistent texting and voicemails.

I wasn't going to take advantage of Mav. Or any of the James brothers for their plane. I hadn't earned it and while I was sleeping with Theo, it wasn't a relationship. He'd made that clear with the whole cum, clean up, and clear out routine. We were nothing like Bridge and Mav.

"Not a chance."

"I'll go with you then," she offered. "Road trip."

I shook my head. "You have school."

"So do you."

"I took it off."

"I'll take it off."

"You can't explain a spontaneous Monday trip to Vegas with me to Mav. Especially when we'll only be in town less than twelve hours. Not happening."

"I'll just tell him it's a secret."

I gave her a look. "Like that's going to go over with him. He'll get the truth out of you one or another."

A flush spread up her cheeks. "Probably true."

"I'll be gone two days and it will be over."

She sighed. Hard. "Fine. But if things go wrong and you need money, you *will* come to me."

I nodded, but that wasn't going to happen. I would not be like Cheryl. I got myself into this mess, I was going to get myself out of it.

36

THEO

THROUGH THE WINDOWS, I'd watched Mallory and Bridget disappear into the depths of the huge house, Scout eagerly following. To talk, I was sure. Women talked a fucking lot. While I stood outside with Mav and Silas staring at a hot grill, I was missing out on time with Mallory. As soon as I saw Bridget back in the kitchen pulling a bowl of potato salad from the fridge, I ditched my brothers, who were arguing over the differences between hickory, oak, and apple wood chips for smoking, and went inside. I didn't cook, nor give a shit about the complex nuances of grilling meat.

I gave a shit about tracking down my woman.

Yeah, she was my woman.

Because when the police rang the doorbell Thursday night at Lindy's house, when she was on my lap and getting her pleasure from my dick, hands and mouth, I'd gone possessive.

No one saw Mallory like I did. Her flared skirt had covered her lower half–and our laps, and her ass, and the fact that my dick was deep inside her. But one tit, glistening, the nipple red and hard from me sucking on it, had been out since I tugged down the cup of her bra.

That alone, just that one perfect bouncing tit exposed, was enough for me to go fucking caveman.

I'd flipped her beneath me–I didn't give a shit if a police officer saw my bare ass–and got her completely covered.

Only then did we answer the door. Of course Mallory knew the guy. Hunter. Named after the town. Or the town was named after his family and his family named him after both. Whatever.

The guy knew it was cool Mallory was in the house and exactly what was up, only smirked and asked if either of us were being murdered. When I gave him a dark look, he smirked some more and told us to quiet down. Then left.

If answering complaint calls about overly loud sex was all the police department had, then this was one boring-ass town. That made it perfect.

Needless to say, it had been a surprise and now I wanted to check and make sure Mallory was okay. By giving her a good, fast fuck. Getting her to a quick–and quiet–orgasm would make me...no, her, feel better.

I found her coming out of one of the ground floor bathrooms. I didn't give her a chance to say a word, just walked her backward right back in there and closed the door behind us, careful not to catch Scout's nose since he was curious and eager to hang with us.

I heard a little disgruntled woof, then his toenails on the wood as he walked away.

"Theo," she whispered, eyes wide at the way I pretty much cavemanned her into the bathroom. I just didn't grab her hair while doing so.

Now she kept her voice down, although it made me hard as fuck remembering *why* she was so loud the day before. Me.

"Wanted to make sure you're okay," I said, stroking her hair, which was down. And silky soft. "After Thursday and all. Didn't get a chance last night."

I'd texted for our usual six o'clock fuck, but she said she was working at her brother's bar, that she was helping him out by filling in. So it'd been almost two days since I got my hands on her. Two long fucking days.

She flushed, clearly just as embarrassed as she'd been the other night. I hadn't been embarrassed. I'd been fucking proud. And I probably owed that guy Hunter a beer.

"I don't want to talk about it."

"Good. Turn around and bend over the sink."

Her mouth fell open. "What? Here? Now?"

"Here. Now. I didn't get you off yesterday, unless you did it yourself with that dildo of yours. I'm sure you know that will never satisfy you like my dick can."

She gasped as I grinned. "How did you know–"

"I didn't, but you just gave yourself away."

"Mav and Bridget are out there! God, Silas, too."

"Don't worry, they don't know about us."

A look I'd never seen before crossed her face, then was

gone. Sadness? No, disappointment? No, discontent? Worry? Who the hell knew? Not me. I pushed on.

"Besides, this is going to be quick, but you're going to have to be quiet. Very, very quiet."

She bit her lip, considered, then turned around.

Fuck, this woman.

My dick was so hard for her. Had been all day.

She set her hands on the edge of the fancy-ass sink, wiggled her hips and stuck her ass out. I glanced at her in the mirror as I tugged down her yoga pants and panties.

I had my dick out and condom covered in seconds, but I didn't immediately push in.

"You wet?

She squirmed as I cupped her from behind. Soaked. Then began to fuck her with two fingers. I watched her in the mirror. Gorgeous. Flushed. Aroused. Fucking mine.

37

MALLORY

I WAS IN BIG TROUBLE. I was close to coming, just from his talented fingers, like that very first night in the restaurant parking lot. My body responded to him like a dog to the rattling of kibble in a bowl. His deep voice asking me if I was wet and I was done for.

Except... it was becoming completely and totally obvious, as if the mirror in front of me showed what was really going on here.

I was getting fucked. Only fucked.

Don't worry, they don't know about us.

I was his dirty little secret. Mav wasn't being discreet by keeping what was going on between me and Theo quiet, he really didn't know his brother and I were having sex. I hadn't told Bridget. Why? *Because it was just sex.* Deep down–and not deep down in my vagina–I'd hoped for more from Theo.

Maybe that was wrong of me, because when I told him my plans of wanting sex with Tom the history teacher, *that* had been just sex. Birth control for smart sex.

Theo had taken that literally when he volunteered.

Smart sex. He used condoms and I was covered by the birth control shot.

But it seemed my vagina and heart were somehow connected, in ways I didn't even know about until all the sexing started, because Theo's words hurt me.

They don't know about us.

He wasn't planning on telling. Or changing my status.

I was now his fuck buddy. Enough where we were doing it sneakily in his brother's bathroom. Or not sneakily and getting the cops called on us.

But it was just sex.

Fudge. The second he tried that Bird of Paradise pose during the yoga class on Tuesday, things changed. I *liked* Theo. No, if I was honest, probably a lot more than liked. He was actually really funny with the driest wit. Kind in a subtle sort of way. Definitely possessive, the way he'd ensured Hunter never saw an inch of me even though he'd gotten an earful. Coming in here, he was checking on me. Perhaps like a guy checks the oil on his car, putting the dipstick in and out, but still. He was asking. And getting ready to put his dipstick in.

Unlike Theo, I wanted Mav and Bridget to know about us. For us to go out there and eat some steaks with Silas and talk about dating. Being a couple. Anything two people did who were into each other. *Besides* sex.

But Theo had different ideas. Or only one.

To sex me up. Satisfy me. I'd wanted to have sex, to

finally not be an almost-virgin any longer. He'd done just that. Was still doing it, and really, really well.

"Ah!" I cried out when he pinched my clit between two fingers. My eyes flew to his in the mirror.

"Where'd you go?" he asked. He was so much bigger than me, a contradiction of uptight and rugged that turned me on. He didn't style his hair any longer. It was a bit longer and unruly now, as if he was finally loosening up. I didn't even want to think about how sexy that beard was, or how it felt between my thighs.

I shook my head, not wanting to tell him. Not only because the truth would definitely drive him away. He wasn't looking for a clingy woman and I wasn't a woman who'd stick around and linger on a guy who wasn't interested. He also had his fingers inside me, rubbing them masterfully over my g-spot in a way that had me panting and clenching around him. Now was *definitely* not the time.

So sex it would be.

"Mav's going to call us to eat anytime," I said. "Think you're skilled enough to get me off before then?"

"Is that a challenge?" One sandy brown brow arched as he questioned me in the mirror. "You know I work best under pressure."

He lined up at my entrance, settled his hands on my hips.

"Do it," I said. *If sex is all I get, let's make it good.*

He thrust in, pressing me against the lip of the pedestal sink and fucked me to not one, but two orgasms so fast, we were back in the kitchen before Mav even brought the burgers inside.

38

THEO

"How long you been fucking Mallory?" Silas asked, putting his seat belt on in the passenger seat of my car.

I put the key in the ignition and glanced his way.

He was serious, but by the curve of his mouth, he was amused.

I glanced at Mav's huge home, the log and stone exterior blending into the mountainside. "A week."

Sex, as in intercourse, not that long, but I didn't think Silas was that technical.

He'd flown in the other night, late, and was staying with me. One thing Bradley had done when we decided to keep the little house Dex had lived in was get the second bedroom furnished. Good thing I'd been with Mallory at Lindy's house instead of at my place on Thursday or Silas would have gotten an eyeful. Better the police showing on a noise complaint than me having to kill my own brother for seeing Mallory bent over the arm of my couch... fuck, or on her knees.

"That's great," he replied. "Never thought I'd see the day you settled into small town life."

I shrugged, started the car. "It's actually not that bad. I made friends with the fire chief and even wowed a roomful of six-year-olds."

"You? Six-year-olds?"

I huffed. "I know. I'm not sure who was more surprised. Me, Mallory, or all those first graders."

"You talked to Mallory's class?"

I nodded.

He chuckled. "Well, Hunter Valley agrees with you. Especially having a little firecracker like Mallory in the sack."

I instantly saw red. I reached out, grasped his jacket. Snarled. "Watch it."

He raised his hands. "Whoa, chill."

I took a deep breath, let it out, then put the car into gear and drove down the street. The pavement was completely clear of snow, even though we'd had about eight inches the other night but was piled along the curb. From what I imagined winter to be like in Hunter Valley, I doubted it would disappear before spring.

"All I mean is she's not Maude. Thank fuck."

I hadn't given Maude a second of thought since I walked into the exam room and found Mallory sitting there in a paper gown. Hell, for months before that. Mallory was my mission. A purpose. And it wasn't saving lives.

It was giving her my dick and all the orgasms that went with it.

Based on the way my balls were drained from the quickie in the bathroom and I was fucking chill–or had been until my brother started poking fun–the mission was a success.

I couldn't get enough of her. My dick was getting hard all over again and wished it was Mallory beside me instead of Silas.

Fuck.

"No one knows. In fact, how do *you* know?"

He turned and gave me a look. "Seriously? You're not very subtle. Even Scout knows."

I had no idea what that meant, especially since dogs didn't talk. Scout might be smart, but he wasn't Lassie. And, Mallory had stayed quiet as she came. We hadn't been in the bathroom long. It was probably the quickest quickie ever. To be honest, I didn't want to know the signs of how unsubtle I was.

I flicked the blinker, then slowed for the turn. "Whatever. It's just sex."

He studied me.

"What? Your sex life so bad you want to talk about mine?"

No way in hell he had a woman. If he did, he wouldn't be in Hunter Valley. He'd be hot and heavy with her right now. But no. He was with me. Then again, I was with him instead of Mallory, which wasn't much better.

He frowned as I pulled into the driveway. "Well played, asshole."

39

MALLORY

"I CAN'T BELIEVE she didn't give you any notice," Lindy said, her voice on speaker.

Bridget and I were in her kitchen eating straight from our own cartons of ice cream. She leaned against the counter by the sink. I was beside the fridge facing her. I had to leave soon to go get ready for the shift at the bar, but for now, we were snacking. We could see Dex's game on the flat screen in the great room. The game was in Boston, so Lindy was alone at their apartment in Denver.

Since Silas and Theo left, Mav headed with Scout to the job site. The James Inn was getting close to being done. The last I heard the interior decorations were being done now.

"She got engaged. It's not like Maggie knew when it was coming." I sighed, jammed the spoon into my container of mint chocolate chip. "I have until the end of the month to move out. I just don't want to listen to them having sex all the time between now and then."

I was such a hypocrite for saying that, considering I'd forced Lindy's old next door neighbor to do the very same thing with me and Theo.

"You're welcome to stay at the house for as long as you want," she offered. "Dex has a game on Thanksgiving in Phoenix, so I'll go with him and enjoy the amazing weather. But we'll be up for Christmas, at least for a few days."

Which meant I had a few weeks to get my shit together, although I really didn't want to stay that long.

I glanced at Bridget, who was licking the Rocky Road from her spoon.

"How did you even know I was there?" I wondered. I hadn't thought about it before. "I was going to call and ask if I could crash for a day or two, but–"

But I was busy having sex with Theo.

"The alarm system."

She'd had it installed before she moved to Denver. Since the house was going to sit empty, she and Dex thought it best if it was monitored. Which meant, so was I.

"And like I said, stay as long as you need. You know you're always welcome."

Gosh, that was such a mom thing to say, and it made me blink back tears.

"The alarm system's supposed to text me when a door or window opens," Lindy continued. "It worked, so thanks for testing that for me."

"Glad I could help," I muttered. Then I wondered what else that alarm system monitored, like emergency calls to the address.

Suddenly, I was done with my ice cream.

If Lindy found out... gah, if Bridge found out about me and Theo, then I was screwed.

Literally, by Theo himself, but figuratively because they couldn't know.

Why? Because what was I going to say? I was casually and thoroughly sexing it up with Mav's brother? That I was using him for his dick?

I couldn't tell them that Theo didn't want more. I wouldn't put them in the middle if he wasn't interested in me for anything *but* sex. Clearly, I wasn't worthy of a relationship. Why would I be? I'd been told all my life I wasn't enough, that I'd never be enough. Without words, Theo proved that.

Didn't that fudging suck?

40

THEO

I PICKED up my phone and sent Mallory a text.

> I have something for you.

Your dick?

> No.

No?

> Well, yes. You can always have my dick.
> But something else.

What is it?

> Be there in an hour.

I couldn't wait to see Mallory's face when she saw her

present. I'd barely kept it a secret the day before when we were at Mav's for lunch. But the paperwork hadn't been signed. Now it was, with a lot of extra cash for the county clerk to push the deed through on the weekend.

Between what she told me about her mom being difficult and having to work shifts at her brother's bar even after her teaching job to save, I wanted to make it easy for her. To take care of her. To take on her troubles and make them go away. Whenever she talked about the little house, she lit up.

So when I took her hand and led her to my car, then drove away from Lindy's house, she was confused. "What is it?" she asked.

I laughed. I hadn't done that enough and it seemed Mallory was pulling them from me. Verna and Jeff, even Mac were all becoming good friends and colleagues, but Mallory... well, she was special.

I had no idea what that even meant.

I slowed in front of the house, then stopped at the curb, eager to share my excitement.

Mallory looked to me, then Mrs. Jonsdottir's place. No, Mallory's.

"Theo, I... what are we doing here?"

"This. This is what I have for you." I turned off the car, climbed out and came around to open her door, but she was already climbing out.

"What?" she asked when we were on the sidewalk.

"Your house," I said, pointing to the little white home. Wasn't it obvious?

I pulled the keys from my coat pocket. "I got you your house."

She stared at the keys, then me.

"You... you got me... my house?"

I took her hand, led her up the shoveled walk. I'd made her speechless, which was probably a first. "Mrs. Jonsdottir was easily swayed with a cash payment. I even offered movers to pack her up and she flew on the James Corp jet this morning to her daughter's in Texas."

"You... you got rid of Mrs. Jonsdottir?"

She followed, but almost tripped on a rise in the concrete where it had buckled a little over the years. That would have to be fixed.

"I didn't get *rid* of her. I just moved her along with a generous incentive. She wanted to be with her family, and you wanted the house."

"How did you know about her family?" she asked, still confused.

"I met with her on Friday."

Since she was standing on the wraparound front porch like she'd been hit on the head with a fly ball, I took the keys back and opened the front door.

When it swung open, the hinges squeaked. Those needed some oil.

Mallory stepped inside.

"It's empty."

"We'll move your things in tomorrow."

She walked around the small living room, stared at the walls, the wood floors, everything. Then back at me.

"You bought Mrs. Jonsdottir's house for me."

I smiled, eager to christen every room in the place. I went over to her, cupped her face and kissed her. "Yes."

She stepped back, looked at me with equal parts horror

and anger. Like one of those Disney villains with horns and smoke coming out of their heads.

"YOU BOUGHT MRS. JONSDOTTIR'S HOUSE FOR ME?" she shouted, her voice echoing off the bare walls.

Oh shit. Clearly, I'd done something wrong. I just had no fucking clue what it might be.

41

MALLORY

"Yes," he repeated, but suddenly not looking quite as confident as he had a few moments ago.

"Why?" I asked, livid. He bought my house. For me. *For* me. He didn't let me do it. He *took* that from me. I was also mad at Mrs. Jonsdottir. She'd promised *me* the house, that she'd reach out to me before anyone else when she finally decided to sell. I'd been saving and even met with Mav's fancy financial planner to grow that nest egg. But no, a huge bank account instead of my shaky stash of cash clearly wasn't much of a debate for her.

"Because you wanted it, and you were working so hard to save for it. The deed's in your name."

I stared at him. Blinked. I wasn't sure if I wanted to strangle him or just walk away. After the past two weeks or so, he hadn't learned a thing about me besides how to get me to come.

Which made me feel like a whore. Not even a high-class call girl like Annie and Trixie.

He was gifting me a fucking house for being a good lay.

"I don't understand why you're so upset," he said, setting his hands on my shoulders.

I shrugged them off.

"Of course, you don't." He was a billionaire. He could buy me the entire town if he wanted. Mrs. Jonsdottir's little house was like pocket change for him. He talked to the woman on Friday, had the cash transferred, the house emptied of her belongings and shipped out of state–along with the woman herself–within forty-eight hours.

"What does that mean?"

I laughed, but it was only the start of tears.

"Whoa, why are you crying?"

"Because!" I tossed my hands in the air. "You took my dream from me!"

His eyes widened and he looked as if I slapped him.

"Took it from you? I *gave* it to you."

I shook my head, let the tears fall. "I don't want it."

"What?" He set his hands on his hips and stared at me like I was crazy. Maybe I was.

"I don't want the house."

"Too bad. It's yours. In your name. I can't do anything with it."

"You–you...oh my God! Fuck!"

"You said this was the one." He glanced around. "Did I buy you the wrong house?"

"Aaaaaaarggghh!" I shouted, then ran out.

He followed. "Mallory!" he shouted as I dashed down the walk. "Where are you going?"

That was the question. I had no idea where I was going. My place with Maggie was mine for only a week or so longer. Lindy's house was just that, *Lindy's* house. I had no place of my own.

Well, now I did, but Theo gave it to me. I wouldn't live in something I hadn't worked for, hadn't earned. I wouldn't turn into my mother, especially from a man who only wanted me for sex. No, this was worse than anything Cheryl did. She'd think I struck the fucking jackpot. A man gave me a house. What would it be next? A car, perhaps.

It was fine to finish off punching my V-card, but now? This? Tom would have probably bought me flowers or maybe a replica of the Sitting Bull monument to put on my desk. Not a house. And Tom wouldn't have given them to me as a token for sexual favors.

"Mallory!"

As I ran down the street, I wondered if Annie ever got a house for those blow job skills she shared with me. Maybe I was better at sex than I ever imagined.

42

THEO

Silas looked over his shoulder at me from his spot on Mav's couch as I came in. "What the fuck is wrong with you?"

Scout circled around me, eager for pets. I reached down, scratched behind his ear.

"Do you guys ever get off the couch?" I asked. When I moved here, I didn't expect them to be such a lazy group.

"Football," Silas and Mav said at the same time.

Bridget lifted her head from Mav's chest where they were sprawled on the long end of the sectional. Football was on. A bag of chips and a bowl of salsa was on the coffee table along with a few beers and cans of soda. "What happened with Mallory?"

I froze, my fingers stilling on Scout. He licked my palm, then gave up. I stood slowly. "Mallory? What do you mean?"

Bridget rolled her eyes. "I didn't think you'd ever play dumb."

I glanced at Mav, who was eyeing me, but not moving from his ridiculously comfortable spot. "I'm with Bridge on this one."

I looked to Silas. He held up a hand. "Didn't say a word."

Bridget pushed up so she sat at Mav's hip, her hand on his stomach. "You don't think we don't know about you two."

"There is no us two," I countered.

Her eyes widened behind her glasses. "That wasn't the two of you having sex in the bathroom?"

I actually felt my neck heat.

"Or whatever it was you two did in the guest bedroom last weekend?"

Now my cheeks were probably bright red.

"Fine. We're having sex. I'm surprised Mallory didn't tell you. You two talk about everything."

"I was letting it play out. Now I know why Tom didn't work out."

"Who's Tom?" Silas asked Bridget.

"A guy who–holy shit," Bridget said, popping up to her feet faster than a meat thermometer in a Thanksgiving turkey.

"Holy shit, what?" Mav wondered, his lax body going tense. Now he got involved since Bridget was freaking out. Scout offered a woof of concern.

Her eyes narrowed. "You knew."

"What?" I asked.

"What?" Mav repeated.

Silas glanced back and forth clearly trying to keep up.

"You knew that Tom had a–that he...you did. You sneaky little–"

"What?" Silas shouted. "And who is Tom?"

"Tom, the history teacher I fixed Mallory up with about two weeks ago. Who bailed at the end of their date. Because Mr. Diarrhea over here knew that Tom had an STD."

Clearly she remembered the reason I ran off that night I was supposed to have dinner with her and Mav.

Silas stared at her as if she needed a reboot. Mav frowned but said nothing. Bridget was a genius with a photographic memory. He knew not to question the accuracy of her words. The clarity, definitely.

"Who is Mr. Diarrhea?" Silas wondered with a grimace.

"How do you know Tom had an STD?" I asked.

"Because he told the gym teacher, he slept with that she should get checked and because she was pissed, she might have gotten chlamydia from him, she got revenge by telling everyone during the inclusivity meeting."

"Let me get this straight," Silas said, sitting up and opening a can of beer that had been on the coffee table. "You set Mallory up with a guy who had chlamydia and it didn't work out for some reason and she ended up having sex with Theo?"

Bridget nodded.

"How did Mallory find out about the STD?" he asked Mallory.

Bridget ignored him and raised an eyebrow at me. "Diarrhea?"

"What's the deal with the shits?" Silas asked, getting frustrated.

"Somehow, Theo knew Tom had a dirty dick and ran out of here to break up the date," Bridget said. She was quiet for a moment as the computer brain of hers worked. "Oh, not Theo, *Dr. James* knew all about it."

I didn't say a word, just went around the table, snagged the full beer from Silas's hand and dropped onto the couch.

"Hey!" Silas muttered.

She was smart, I'd give her that.

"Okay, so you had this Tom guy as a patient and can't say a word. I have to admit, brother, your privacy skills are impressive." Silas then looked at Bridget. "That all makes sense, but what's the deal with diarrhea?"

I looked to Silas. "Do you really want to know?"

He studied me, considered it. Did anyone really want to know a diarrhea story unless you were seven? It was right up there with farts. "No."

Mav only laughed, pulled Bridget down on top of him and gave her a kiss. "You should work with Hunter at the police station. Your detective skills are impressive."

Hunter. Fuck. The guy who'd interrupted me and Mallory.

"Back to Mallory. Why did you come in here all pissed?" Silas asked. "I know I don't live here and all, but I'm trying to keep up. It's really fucking complicated for small town life."

"Move here," Bridget said earnestly.

Silas laughed as if the idea was ridiculous.

"I bought her a gift and she didn't like it," I answered.

"That's not like her," Bridget responded with a frown. "Mallory loves cute things. What did you get her? A necklace? Lingerie? Those cute fuzzy socks she always wears around the house?"

I shook my head. "A house."

43

THEO

I STUCK my head in the door of Room 314, Bridget's physics classroom, just as a bell rang. All of a sudden, it was like a stampede of wild teenagers. I stepped back so I didn't get trampled.

As the room emptied, the hall filled and I moved inside.

Bridget was behind her desk organizing papers.

"I think I like six-year-olds better," I said, when I watched the swarm of students moving around in the hallway. They were loud, obnoxious and made me slightly fearful of our future.

But then I remembered what Silas, Mav, and I were like at that age. Dex had been little then, like those six-year-olds and their missing teeth.

Bridget looked up, grinned. "I'm surprised they let you in."

I tapped the sticker I'd slapped on my shirt that

indicated I was a visitor. "I had to show my ID and explain how I knew you. I was expecting to give a urine sample but coincidentally Tom the history teacher was checking his mailbox and vouched for me."

She pushed her glasses up and grinned. "The gym teacher is ruthless."

"Remind me not to date her."

She frowned and gave me a slightly dirty look. Dirty as in she wanted to kill me with a rusty butter knife. "I thought you were dating Mallory."

I shook my head. "We're not dating."

"Just having sex."

"Exactly."

"This is lunch period, so you aren't here for physics. What's up?"

"Where's Mallory?" I asked. *That* was the reason for my impromptu stop at Hunter Valley High School.

"I thought you're not dating."

"We're not. She missed our usual six o'clock visit last night."

She put the papers down, turned and leaned against her desk. Then she changed her mind and crossed the room to shut the door. The hallway had settled down, probably because everyone was in the cafeteria. Crossing her arms over her chest, she looked–at least tried–to look formidable. She was too small to be anything but a little scary. Like a honey badger with glasses.

"You have a standing sex time?"

"Don't you with Mav?"

Her mouth dropped open. "You actually do?"

"Yes."

"Oh my God, Theo." She closed her eyes for a moment, then came over and patted my chest. "You need help."

"I know. Where's Mallory? She's not answering any of my texts and she was obviously–and strangely–angry about the house."

"Out of town."

"What do you mean out of town? She was in town yesterday."

"Yeah, when you showed her the house you bought for her." She sighed. "Look, she's not a patient you see at a certain time, examine them then send on their way. Wait, you get what I mean. I'm not saying that you have sex with patients. I'm saying you can't treat Mallory like you're providing her a service."

"But–"

"I get it. She wanted sex. You gave it to her instead of Tom and his dirty dick."

"Exactly."

"But it changed. You bought her a house."

"Right."

"You have feelings for her."

I shook my head.

"You tackled entering high school, which is like a modern day fortress, just to ask me where Mallory is."

"Right."

She studied me as I wondered why we were talking in circles. "For a guy who's so smart, you are the biggest doofus I've ever met."

"I'm not sure if I should be offended or wait for you to clarify."

With a huff and a shake of her head, she finally said,

"You and Mallory are perfect for each other. Stubborn. Prideful. Idiots."

I realized this was one of those times where I should remain silent.

"Okay. Let's see how this shakes out. Remember you have my back when she hates me later this week."

I blinked. "I don't know what that means. Is it some kind of girl code?"

"Like the *diarrhea* is for boys?" she countered.

I couldn't help but grin at her witty reply.

"Mallory is in"—she glanced at the clock on the wall– "or almost in, Las Vegas for a court appearance tomorrow morning."

"That is the last thing I expected you to say." She remained silent. "Court hearing for what?"

She shook her head. "She has to tell you that."

Before I moved out of Mav's house, it was distinctly possible I heard him spank Bridget. As a kink. But still, I wished Mav was here to give her a spanking now to talk. Why the hell would Mallory have a court appearance in Las Vegas? She'd been there... last weekend? Not even two weeks ago. Oh fuck. What the hell happened to her on that trip? I knew bachelor parties went a little wild, but Mallory in Vegas for a bachelorette weekend?

Oh shit. Anything could be possible.

"She won't answer my texts," I countered when there was no way I could ask her about it if she didn't respond.

Bridget threw her hands up in the air, then pointed at the door. "Get out of my classroom. If you can operate on a dying person, you can figure this out on your own from here."

44

MALLORY

"THANKS again for letting me stay here. You have an amazing place." I took in the floor to ceiling window with views of the Vegas mountains, whatever they were called. There was even a flipping cactus in the back lawn by a sparkling, kidney shaped pool. *This* was impressive. I was all for women-driven businesses and it seemed Annie was quite the entrepreneur. I certainly wouldn't ding her for her profession. Girl power all the way.

I seemed to have the knack for BJs, based on Theo's response to my efforts. And he'd kept things completely and totally unattached, important for this line of work. Maybe I should rethink my role of educating the young of tomorrow.

Annie led me into the foyer–yes, it was fancy enough to be more than an entry–and gave me a reassuring smile. "No problem. Trixie said she's bringing dinner in a little while.

In the meantime, I want to hear about the guy and the tips and if you used any of them."

I'd driven for thirteen hours–and thought way too hard about Theo and my life–and was equally exhausted and hyped up on gas station coffee. I felt as rough as I probably looked, while Annie was, of course, stunning. As if she rolled out of bed like this. Her red hair was styled and she had makeup on and her casual outfit was too perfect to be anything but intentional. I wearily dropped my bag, which only included an outfit and makeup for my court appearance and a nightshirt, wondering if I'd be in an orange jumpsuit by this time tomorrow.

"The guy? I gave him a BJ using all your tips. After, he bought me a house, so I think you could teach a class."

Then I burst into tears.

THEO

> I know you're in Vegas for a court
> appearance. Call me.

I'd texted Mallory, but she hadn't responded. Not once.

I paced across the office, which wasn't far, then turned around. I was between patients, checking messages like a high schooler.

The phone out in the lobby rang and I heard Verna answer.

Mallory wasn't calling back. Why the fuck wasn't she calling? Oh yeah, she was mad because I bought her a house. Why wouldn't she be happy with a fucking house? Her *dream* house at that. Well, I was mad at her for not telling me she had a court appearance in fucking Las Vegas.

What the fuck?

I turned, stared at my cell sitting on my desk. Still nothing.

Fuck!

Bridget hadn't been any fucking help earlier, going so far as to kick me out of her classroom. I couldn't believe it!

Mallory could be on the side of the road in the middle of Utah, car broken down. I'd seen her car. Not the newest model, but it wasn't on its last legs either. Still. Alone on the side of the highway? All kinds of shit could happen. No. She'd have called Bridget if there was a problem. Right?

Why had she gone alone in Vegas anyway? Bridget was supposed to be her best friend.

WHAT HAD MALLORY DONE?

I ran a hand over my beard.

"What is going on with you?" Verna asked. "Did you drink the killer, death inducing coffee that Steaming Hotties has? That stuff has triple the caffeine. Next, you're going to be climbing the walls or having a heart attack."

I spun around and glared at Verna in the doorway.

"Why would someone have a court appearance?" I asked, running my hand through my hair, then setting it on my hips.

Her eyes widened, but she remained as calm as ever. "Okay, so I'll call Eve at Steaming Hotties and be sure you're on the Do Not Serve list for that stuff."

"Verna," I said. "You're wise to all things. Help."

"Wow. Um... okay." She tapped her chin in sync with me tapping my toe on the floor.

"Reasons for a court appearance. Hmm. Getting divorced."

Mallory was not getting divorced. I shook my head.

"Child custody hearing?"

"Definitely not."

She shrugged. "The only other thing I can think of is getting arrested."

"That's–" Arrested? Mallory? There was no way she'd be that impulsive or reckless or crazy to do something that had her thrown in jail.

No, she totally was.

"Holy fuck."

"Um..."

I took the stethoscope from around my neck and set it on my desk. I went over to Verna, set a hand on her arm. "There's no one dying, right?"

She frowned. "Um... no."

"Good. I have to go."

46

MALLORY

W<small>HEN</small> I <small>SAW</small> Theo's text, that he knew I was in Las Vegas and why, I showed it to Annie and Trixie. I had a box of tissues in hand, and I had barely stopped crying in hours. They'd laughed and told me not to worry, that if I didn't have a gag reflex and did yoga, Theo wouldn't be done with me.

From their perspective, it made sense. The men they spent time with found both of those things as important job requirements. I didn't want Theo to be a customer and with Mrs. Jonsdottir's house in my name, he couldn't be anything else.

I wasn't sure what I was more panicked and upset about. Being found guilty for solicitation or feeling like I was paid for sex by Theo. God, if the judge only knew that a man bought me a house for services rendered, I'd be found guilty.

That was why I had to give the house back. When Trixie arrived with bags of carry out, I explained what I had to do. The women weren't so sure, because why would a woman turn down a house? It was protection. A place to live where no one could take away.

It was exactly what I always wanted. Not just that specific house, but a place of my own. Where Maggie wouldn't be choosing Nate over me. Where I never came in last.

But Theo gave it to me just like I gave my mother the money for the utility bill. I was struggling and he took care of the problem. But what about the next time when my car needed new tires? Would he pay for that, too? Was I just someone he pitied? I specifically told him that night in the restaurant parking lot that I didn't want pity sex. I would *not* be a charity case like my mother, always assuming others would solve her financial problems.

Where she used my need for attention and affection as a weapon, offering it sparingly and strategically.

Theo gave me affection, at least in the form of sex. Sparingly. Strategically, as in at six o'clock. His sex hour.

I would not try to get scrapes of affection from Theo that would never come. Well, it seemed I'd tried for them, but it had never come. Only a house. A house was not an indication of any kind of feeling on his part. Annie and Trixie could confirm that.

The other proof? We barely kissed!

I told the ladies as much and they must have recognized how serious I was, how important to me getting rid of that house meant, so they got their lawyer on the phone in a total speed dial move. The pertinent details were shared and within the hour, Annalynn, their ever efficient lawyer, arrived with the paperwork for me to give the house back to Theo before we finished our dinner and first glasses of wine.

She couldn't have been over thirty and dressed like she was on a legal drama on TV. Form-fitting, modest but bold dress and killer heels. Simple makeup and a personality of a diplomatic shark.

I learned the plat and other fancy information about the house was public record, so all I had to do was sit at Annie's fancy kitchen counter and sign the document. Annalynn even notarized it.

She tucked the paper in an express mail envelope.

"That's it?" I asked, watching her in awe as it was sealed shut.

"Quit claim deeds are simple," she explained. "You're signing the deed of ownership over to someone else. Usually it's to a family member, but it works in a case like yours. No money's changing hands, just the property itself."

She smiled and I had to wonder what shade lipstick she used. She lifted the envelope. "This will be at the courthouse in Hunter Valley tomorrow morning and the deed recorded by lunch."

Before I even returned home, the house would belong to Theo. Just like that.

I blinked. "Wow. Um... thanks."

She eyed me with a soft smile. "You must really love this guy."

I blinked my still-swollen eyes in her direction. "I don't love him."

The corner of her mouth tipped up. "I've dealt with

plenty of divorces. No woman would return a house to a man if she hated him."

Trixie nodded, tipped her glass of wine at Annalynn. "That's true."

"There's no marriage. No divorce. That makes no sense."

"Neither does love, honey. Neither does love." Annalynn cocked her head to the side, studied me. "You okay?"

Was I okay? Hell, no. I laughed.

"I feel like I've got PMS times ten. Relieved, sad." Because Theo didn't care about me like I cared about him. "Worried." Because maybe Annalynn was right. Maybe I was falling for him. "Panicked." Not just because I might be off to jail, but my feelings for Theo? Holy sugar and spice. I did have feelings for him, but he had none for me in return. "Tired. And I'm pretty sure eating junk food in the car made my pants not fit."

"You worry too much. If you could stay longer, we'd do a spa day," Trixie offered.

"That sounds amazing, but I can't. I have to be back at work. And that means I can't be found guilty because I *will* lose my job and in a small town like Hunter Valley, I'll be known as the Vegas hooker." I looked to Annie and Trixie. "No offense."

They laughed and Trixie said, "The judge is going to take one look at you and toss the case."

I had no idea what that meant. I could look sophisticated and sexy, couldn't I? I knew all about sex now, thanks to Theo and I gave house-buying worthy BJs.

Maybe it was my sloppy hair and coffee stained Hunter Valley Elementary hoodie I had on.

"Like Trixie said, the charges against you will be dropped," Annalynn promised.

And they were. Annalynn was a pro–no pun intended–at handling my court appearance and the next morning the whole thing was over within ten minutes. The judge threw out my case because there was no probable cause. She also took in my outfit, heard about my residence in Montana and my job as a first-grade teacher and she actually rolled her eyes. She dropped the gavel, and it was over.

I turned to Annie and Trixie, who were seated in the long benches behind me, the entire courtroom looking just like on TV. Annie winked and offered a thumbs up while Trixie only grinned. I was practically shaking in relief.

Annie's and Trixie's hearings followed soon after mine and they, too, were cleared, although they both were given fines. Based on Annie's fancy house and the way they barely blinked at the sum announced by the judge, the amount wasn't an issue. Maybe they could expense it on her tax returns.

As for me, I was thrilled to be back to being only a boring first-grade teacher without a record, able to get my bail back to give to Bridge for the plane ticket.

We walked out of the courthouse free women, and I had to admit, their easy joy was infectious. I'd been so anxious about the whole thing, and it felt like a weight was lifted from my shoulders.

"Come on, let's get some lunch before you go," Annie offered. "We never really got a chance to hear about the–"

"Theo," I gasped. People coming out of the courthouse

had to part to walk around us because I froze mid-step. There, standing ten feet in front of me was the man himself.

I wasn't sure if I wanted to run away or run into his arms.

I chose running away.

47

THEO

I was prepared for Mallory to be surprised at seeing me but taking off like a sprinter in the Olympic hundred-meter dash was a surprise. Since she wasn't a professional athlete and was wearing heels, she didn't get very far before I caught up with her.

With one hand hooked about her waist, I stopped her. The hot Vegas sun beat down on us and I was sweating.

"Easy, tiger," I murmured in her ear. I felt her ragged breathing, the shaking. She was nervous. Afraid. When her eyes met mine, I realized she wasn't afraid. She was mad.

"What are you *doing* here?" she hissed. Her cheeks were flushed but not from the sun.

She just stared at me, more like gave me a death glare.

"To see you. What are *you* doing here?" I countered.

Her lips pinched together so tightly. It was clear she had no intention of responding.

"This must be Theo." The three women who came out of the courthouse with Mallory approached. It was the redhead who spoke.

Her gaze was laser sharp and scanned my body in a way that hadn't happened to me before. I had a feeling she'd cataloged my net worth, my body mass index and my dick size in two seconds.

What I picked up was she was stunningly beautiful and knew my name. That meant Mallory mentioned me.

I didn't let go of Mallory as I shifted us to face her friends. "Yes. And you are?"

Maybe I could glean some information out of them.

"I'm Annie." She set her hand on her bountiful breasts that even a conservative white blouse couldn't disguise. The strategic motion was to drive my eyes to her assets in a subtle but very direct way. "This is Trixie and Annalynn."

I nodded. "Ladies."

"Everything makes sense now, Mal," the blonde introduced as Trixie said. She was also exquisitely pretty. Tall and slim. Elegant. Their clothes were expensive and everything about them screamed high-class.

The third, Annalynn, nodded in agreement. There was no question she was a lawyer. It was as if her profession was stamped on her forehead. From her conservative and very business-like attire to the way she held herself. She also carried a briefcase. I didn't know anyone else who used one–and James Corp had a slew of lawyers in house and on retainer.

"What makes sense?" I asked.

"Nothing," Mallory replied, giving the women an imploring look.

"Are you her friends from the bachelorette party?" If I had to pull answers from them like a dentist pulled teeth, I would. "Which one of you is getting married?" I asked.

Annie looked to Trixie. Trixie looked at Annie. They laughed.

So not her college friends.

"How did your court appearance go?" I prodded, hoping that the other women would think I knew what was going on. Which I sure as hell didn't.

"Your girlfriend's case was dropped. She no longer needs to change her profession, but from what I heard" – Trixie looked down my body and blue eyes stopped squarely on my crotch– "she's a natural."

I frowned and shifted Mallory in front of me–I hadn't let go of her waist–to block the woman from imagining what my dick looked like.

"Natural?"

"Call girl," Annie said with a throaty laugh. "Didn't you know? Your girl Mallory is a professional call girl."

Mallory? Mallory Mornay? The goofy first-grade teacher? The one with the duck socks, had a body made for sin, who fucked like a porn star and gave head like–

A professional call girl.

What. The. Actual. Fuck?

48

MALLORY

"I AM *NOT* A CALL GIRL," I said, stating it loudly and plainly. Too loudly since a few heads turned in our direction.

That statement was for Annie, who was messing everything up, to her amusement. And that of Annalynn and Trixie as well.

One glance at Theo and it seemed he might be doubting me. I flushed hotly remembering what I did to him have him think twice.

"We are," Trixie said proudly, pointing between Annie and herself.

Inwardly, I groaned. It seemed women who bared their bodies for work had no issue with baring their secrets either.

"Yes, I got pointers when we were in the holding cell," I admitted, then bit my lip. I'd said too much.

Annie all but preened.

"Holding cell?" Theo asked, eyes going wide. "You were arrested?"

I rolled mine.

Trixie huffed out a laugh. "I can see you two don't do much talking." Then she eyed Theo like she would a chocolate cake. "Not that I blame you."

Annie nodded. "Why waste time talking when you can do other things?"

"Ladies, I have another appointment. Good luck, Mallory," Annalynn said, holding out her hand. I shook it. "Call me if you need help with another arrest... or other paperwork."

"I think I'm a one-and-done client, but thanks." I knew my cheeks were on fire. This was not going well. Not at all.

Theo turned me toward him as Annalynn disappeared back inside the building. "Arrest? Holding cell? Call girl?"

I swallowed, closed my eyes briefly, then tugged up my big girl panties.

"Yes. I was arrested for solicitation."

Theo laughed. Head tipped back, deep and long.

The fuc–flipping jerk.

"Why are you laughing?" I asked, angry all over again.

He actually wiped his eye. "You? Solicitation? A hooker?"

Annie and Trixie stepped back once, then again, as if they knew the kraken was about to be unleashed.

The kraken was me.

I crossed my arms over my chest and narrowed my eyes.

"You're the one that died for a minute when I had your dick down my throat and a finger in your ass." I lowered my voice so I didn't announce it to everyone in front of the building, but Annie and Trixie heard.

Theo's jaw clenched and his cheeks flushed.

"You did the finger trick?" Annie asked, tapping Trixie on the arm and they nodded at each other. "I told you it would go over well. That's my girl."

For the first time in... forever, I was proud of myself.

I stepped closer and poked Theo in the chest. "Why is it that a Las Vegas call girl believes in me more than you?"

His mouth fell open, then he snapped it shut. He was quiet for a moment as he studied me, then turned to Annie. "She's got the perfect mix of sweet and pure sin, doesn't she? I'm sure a call girl with that personality would be a hit."

Annie and Trixie nodded in unison.

"I speak for my dick when I personally thank you for sharing your tips with Mallory."

"Oh my go–sh," I said, slapping my hands over my face, as if that was going to make me disappear.

"I assume since you're not in custody that the charges were dropped?"

"Yes," I said into my fingers.

He nodded. "Good. We need to go. The plane is waiting for us to return to Hunter Valley."

I dropped my hands and stared at Theo. Of course he took his plane to get here.

"You came to give me a ride back to Hunter Valley."

He nodded.

That was the reason he was here. A ride. Maybe it was generosity, or chivalry. But it wasn't concern. Or worry. He didn't *care* about me, only that I got back safe. It was the doctor in him. Right?

"Plane?" Annie asked. "Mal, you hit the jackpot on the first pull."

"I'm driving back," I told Theo.

He shook his head as if I was crazy. No one turned down a private plane for a thirteen-hour car ride. "I have the plane."

"*The* plane," Annie repeated, nudging Trixie.

"I have my car here. I can't leave it here. I have to drive it back." And I didn't want to take anything else from him.

Theo considered something, then nodded. "Looks like it'll be a road trip then."

Um... what?

49

THEO

W<small>E WERE</small> an hour outside of Vegas in a remote section of Nevada that looked like a sandbox. Dusty brown hills. Not a spec of water or greenery, except for small patches around popup motels or fast food restaurants clustered at the highway exits.

I stood in front of a clump of this greenery, squinting against the bright sun at a random palm tree. Mallory had made me pull into a truckstop so she could change out of the dress clothes she wore to court, to grab snacks and take a bathroom break. She was inside now choosing processed snacks loaded with salt and hydrogenated palm oil while I baked in the hot sun. I'd planned to be in Vegas long enough to grab Mallory. Back and forth from Montana in a few hours. I wasn't even dressed right for the hot weather.

"You've never been on a road trip before, have you?"

I spun around at Mallory's voice, took in the food she

hugged against her body. Chips. Candy. Drinks. "That stuff is going to kill you."

She glanced down at the stash, then back at me. She wore sunglasses, so her pale eyes were hidden. "Yeah, no road trip for you. Snacks are a requirement. How old are you? Forty?"

I gave her a steely look. "Thirty-six."

She paused, studied me. "You seem much older."

"Thirty-six," I said through gritted teeth.

"Well, I can't believe you made it this long without one."

"I have a plane."

"Right." She reached out and handed me sunglasses I hadn't noticed since her arms were so full. "Here."

I took them automatically. "What are these for?"

"We're in the desert. It's bright. You're driving." She shook her head. "How did you get through medical school again?"

The shades were a cheap truckstop throwback to the eighties. Thick plastic frames. In electric blue.

I put them on. Fuck, that was better.

She pinched her lips together to hide a smile. I had no doubt I looked like an idiot. Being in the middle of that desert she mentioned, I didn't really give a shit. "Lookin' good."

"Thanks."

She went to the driver's side.

"What the hell are you doing?" I asked, crossing over to her and blocking her from opening the car door.

"What?"

The hot wind ruffled her hair, which was pulled up in a sloppy bun. Since Mallory had driven her car to the courthouse with the intention of leaving from there to drive back to Montana, it had made it easy for us to get on the road. But her wardrobe hadn't been a comfortable option. She entered the truck stop like she was ready for a middle management job interview and came out looking...like Mallory. She was dressed down in another pair of those stretchy yoga pants and a short-sleeved Silvermines t-shirt. Fuck, those pants and her ass. And that shirt and her tits.

"You're not driving."

"It's my car."

"You're not driving."

She stared at me. I stared at her. And waited.

She huffed, then turned on her sneakered heel to go around the car. "Fine."

We were back on the road, and she was breaking open a tube of formed potato chips. Horrible music blasted from the stereo. I pushed the scan button. Radio stations were few and far between. The next one that came up was a religious sermon. I hit scan again. It circled all the way around to the original station.

"I can't believe Bridget told you about my arrest." With her ridiculous flexibility, she put her feet up on the dash. I imagined them like that but wrapped around my waist. Inwardly, I groaned. This drive was going to be fucking long for so many reasons.

"She didn't," I said as I checked in the rearview mirror so I didn't keep ogling those toned thighs.

She froze with a chip halfway to her mouth. "Then how *did* you know I was in Vegas?"

"She told me you had a court appearance. Nothing more. I think it's time for you to fill in some blanks."

Shoving a few chips in her mouth wouldn't stall her for long. The canister was only so deep and we had hours to go.

"Fine," she said finally.

I was quickly learning that *fine* didn't mean that anything was actually fine.

She handed me the canister. "If we're going to do this, then you need some chips."

If it would get her to talk, then I'd eat some heart clogging chips. I stuck my hand in, grabbed a small stack and set them on my jean-clad thigh.

The blue sky was crisscrossed with contrails from planes going in and out of Las Vegas. I had to wonder if one of them was the James Corp jet returning to Hunter Valley without us.

"I flirted with a guy who turned out to be an undercover cop. He arrested me," she explained.

"Flirting doesn't indicate you're a hooker."

"I prefer call girl. It's much more high-class," she countered.

I couldn't help but grin. I shoved a chip in my mouth. The salty taste was... really good.

I shoved in another.

"Fine. Call girl," I said with a mouthful of chips.

She went on to detail how she'd pushed the guy on his price, and it made me laugh. When Mallory realized I was laughing *with* her instead of *at* her, she smiled too.

"The undercover officer must have been blind. No way he'd mistake you for a hooker." If she dressed up that night as she did for her court appearance, I couldn't imagine how the guy would ever even walk up to her in a sting.

"Hey!" She grabbed her cell out of her purse, slid her finger over it for twenty seconds or more. "Here."

She held out the phone so I could glance at it while driving. It was a photo of Mallory and three other women. It had clearly been taken in a casino, with slot machines in the background. All four were in dresses leaning toward slutty on the appropriate meter. I glanced at the road, then at Mallory in the image. She looked gorgeous in the dark green sleeveless dress and she in no way looked like middle management.

Fuck, she was pretty. And now I was hard. I shifted in the seat as Mallory put her cell away.

"The officer wasn't blind," I admitted. "You definitely looked like a call girl. A high-class one at that."

"Hey!" she said again, as if I'd insulted her again.

"Easy, tiger. You get mad when I don't think you look like a call girl, and you get mad when I say you do."

She huffed, shoved a chip in her mouth, then grudgingly said, "You're right."

She opened a bottle of some kind of iced tea and handed it to me. I gave the label a quick peek before taking a sip. Peach. Not bad.

"Let me get this straight," I said, handing the bottle back where she took a swig herself. "You were in a holding cell and befriended two hoo– call girls and they gave you sex tips which you used on me."

"Yes."

"The blow job," I said, then got instantly hard thinking about how insanely fucking incredible it had been.

"Oh, look!" she pointed at a swiftly approaching billboard. "A dinosaur site in five miles. Let's stop."

We were talking about her sex talents, and she wasn't even focusing.

"Why didn't you tell me about any of this?" I asked.

"Why? Because it was my problem."

I frowned. "So? So I'd have offered the plane and we wouldn't be out in the middle of nowhere."

"Exactly. This was a mess I needed to fix on my own. Besides, the less people who knew about what happened the better. If it got out what happened, I could have been fired."

"I'm not *people*, I'm–" I was going to say *your man,* but that was wrong. "I'm a doctor. I can keep things confidential." Like chlamydia patients.

She shook her head. "I won't be beholden."

"Beholden? Was that blind date of yours an English Lit teacher?"

She rolled her eyes.

"I won't be like my mother."

Oh. Well, I hadn't met the woman, but I really didn't like her.

"She still bothering you?"

A shrug and a swig of tea was all the response I got. It seemed I couldn't help her with that, either.

As she said, *fine.*

"Ooh, I love this song!" she cooed, reaching for the volume and turning it up, tapping her toes on the dash as she sang along. I'd never heard it before in my life.

This woman was a complete dichotomy. Junk food eating, sweet first-grade teacher with attachment issues, a fascination for weird side-of-the road tourist traps who sucked dick like a porn star and was just all around...

happy. Maybe it was avoiding jail time that helped with that.

I took in the terrain. It looked like Mars, but hot. No one was around. A car was ahead of us about a half mile. Glancing in the rearview mirror, there was an eighteen-wheeler cruising a way behind us.

This stretch of road was deserted as hell and I had the cruise control set to eighty-five. I imagined Mallory driving this all alone and clenched the steering wheel. Instead of blowing past the exit–which seemed like nothing more than ranch access–I blinkered, for no other reason than abiding by the law, and took it.

She swiveled her head around. "This isn't the exit for the dinosaur thing."

I didn't say a word, only turned right off the top of the exit ramp, then pulled over on the side of the dirt road about a quarter mile down. Shut off the car and the radio fell blissfully silent. I took off my seatbelt.

"I'll stay in the car while you pee," she offered.

I shifted my leg to face Mallory, grabbed the canister of chips and set it on the floor at her feet, screwed the lid on the tea, then unclipped her belt.

"I don't have to pee."

I didn't know why I was brooding or bothered that she could've been out here all alone. Or that she hadn't confided in me about her arrest. This was Mallory and this was just about sex. With sex, we were in agreement. We liked it hot. We liked it often. We liked it really fucking dirty.

"Ever fuck in a car before?"

Her eyes widened–I could tell even behind her sunglasses–and she glanced around, then back at me.

She shook her head and a sly smile spread across her face.

"Show me what else you learned from your friends," I ordered.

"You really want to know?"

"Show, not know, tiger."

She tapped her lip as if she had multiple possibilities she was considering. "Push your seat back."

Reaching down between my legs, I grabbed the metal bar and did as she requested.

Then she crawled over the center console and into my lap.

"Get ready, doctor, to have your world rocked."

50

MALLORY

THEO PULLED into Lindy's driveway after midnight. I was exhausted and my ass was numb. I climbed out, reached my arms overhead and stretched. Compared to Las Vegas, the air in Hunter Valley was crisp and biting cold. I shivered as Theo came around the car.

"Thanks for driving. The entire way." I hadn't wanted him to join me. I hadn't even wanted him to show up in Vegas. Or know anything about what happened. But I had to admit, he made the drive easier. And the sex had certainly been a fun break.

He nodded. "Come on. Let's get some sleep."

I looked at him, then the front door, then him again. Maybe my brain was too tired to understand. "You want to stay here?"

He'd never slept over before. Or me in reverse. Not once.

"My car's not here," he explained. "I'm not walking and I'm more tired than I remember ever being in residency. Then I stayed up for thirty-six hours straight."

Oh. Well, that made un-romantic sense. He was staying with me out of necessity, not desire.

Like the house. Like his appearance in Vegas. Like right now. But somehow, even with all that, I felt closer to him. Road trips didn't give anyone a choice in that. It was really a dangerous feeling.

"Road trips take it out of you," I replied like I did with a student's parents who sucked at their role, but I couldn't outright tell them.

He grunted, slung a heavy arm over my shoulder and walked with me to the door.

I let us in, climbed the stairs and pointed to Bridge's bed. He was already toeing off his shoes.

"If you'd let me drive at all, you wouldn't be so tired," I reminded.

He only grunted in response.

As I closed the door to the bathroom to brush my teeth and at least wash the miles off my face, Theo yanked back the covers and fell face first onto the bed. He groaned in satisfaction—a very similar sound to the one I pulled from him when I rode his dick, reverse cowgirl, in the car earlier.

Five minutes later, I climbed in with a sleeping Theo. With him on his stomach, he was a bed hog. I pushed at him, and he turned, reached out and tucked me into his side. All without really waking up.

He was warm and cozy, and I took a moment to enjoy the feel of him. We never lingered in bed. I'd never been able to just... be with him. I took in his scent. A hint of his cologne still lingered along with stale coffee from when he'd spilled some on his shirt somewhere in Idaho. His heart thumped beneath my hand.

This man was solid. Sturdy.

He'd come to Las Vegas for me. Even, perhaps especially, because he didn't know *why* I had a court appearance. He up and flew to me.

I smiled against his chest. I didn't know what was up with him, but all I felt was relief. No longer the chance of being a convicted hooker. No longer a homeowner of a place I hadn't gotten myself. From what Annalynn had said, the house was now in Theo's name. It didn't belong to me any longer. I wasn't *beholden* to him.

I felt like things had changed. I felt... more. A glimmer. Something more than just sex. I was getting my shit together, one thing at a time. No more possible criminal record. No more owing Bridge.

So I didn't have Mrs. Jonsdottir's house. I'd had it and it felt wrong. Like it wasn't mine. It wasn't. I'd move my things out of Maggie's apartment and put them in Lindy's garage. For the time being, I'd save a little on having no rent while I found just the right place, socking more money into the down payment fund. I could maybe... let someone in. Maybe?

I'd been angry at Theo when he'd magically appeared at the courthouse. Stuck with him in a car all day made that go away. The orgasms in the car had helped. So was being in his arms right now.

Theo sniffled, then twitched once. I couldn't help but

smile. This moment of quiet made me want to open my heart to him. To have more times like this–perhaps when he was conscious–when he held me solely because he wanted to.

I fell asleep for the first time in a man's arms. All I knew was that I was glad it was Theo.

51

THEO

I woke up with Mallory's ass against my dick and her hair in my mouth. Both were a first. Mallory, yes. But waking up to a woman in my bed, that was new, especially close enough to feel her lush curves and choke on her silky strands. I took women to bed, but they never stayed in mine. Or I in hers.

This was actually Bridget's bed, so perhaps it was like the Switzerland of sleeping. Neutral turf.

Except I was fully clothed, and Mallory was in a long shirt which had ridden up. She was warm and soft and silent.

No *fine*. No loud singing every lyric to every song across the state of Utah. No laughing. Or moaning. Just her.

My arm was slung over her waist and my nose was buried in her soft hair. I didn't want to move my hand, but I had to clear my mouth. I kissed the top of her head. I...

liked this. Liked holding her. Ridiculously enough, I'd liked the road trip. I felt a connection. A change in us. That she was beginning to understand our dynamic.

So we had sex in the car when it wasn't scheduled. So I ate some deliciously bad for me food. I was learning how to have fun.

I was actually, strangely, having fun.

This could work, me and Mallory. She'd come over later for *sex* o'clock. I smiled at my play on time. She wouldn't be stressed or worried about a thing. She had her house, no arrest looming. I fixed her problems. I–

Her cell phone's alarm clock blared, as loud as the music from the car ride.

"Fuck," I muttered.

She jolted, then groaned. Then froze. Then tried to wiggle, which only brought her ass against my dick.

"Easy, tiger."

When she moved again, I lifted my arm and she popped from bed.

"I have school."

I glanced up at her, hair a mess, eyes more asleep than awake. The pale blue nightshirt that may have covered her tits but didn't do a thing to hide the full swells or the plump tips. Even though I knew *exactly* what they looked like, there was something unbelievably sexy about this look. Intimate.

Fuck, I was hard. So hard it hurt. I knew what could fix that.

"I know you usually come over at six, but how about six am instead of six pm?" I asked, reaching down and rubbing my dick through my jeans.

Her gaze dropped to watch what my hand was doing. I was fully clothed in my day-old outfit and she looked at me as if I was one of those male revue dancers.

She shook her head, as if to clear away cobwebs. "I have to shower." Lifting her sleep shirt up and over her head, she tossed it aside so she was only in a pair of pale pink panties. With a glance over her shoulder, she added, "But I can multitask."

I hopped from the bed and followed her across the hall into the bathroom while I tugged down the zipper on my jeans. "I'm a trauma surgeon. Multitask is my middle name."

52

THEO

"WHAT'S WRONG?" Verna asked.

I froze, patted my stethoscope around my neck automatically. Looked around. "Nothing. Why?"

"You're smiling," she said, her voice laced with suspicion.

I laughed.

"Now you're laughing." She stood from her seat at her desk and came around the counter. She held an instant read thermometer.

I held up my hands to ward her off, forcing the smile from my face. "I'm fine."

"You were gone for a day and a half and now you're... happy."

I wasn't sure about that. "No one's died this week."

"*That's* what makes you happy?" she asked, clearly concerned.

I frowned. "Aren't you glad no one's died?"

She shrugged. "Sure, but it's not something I take time to consider. I mean, it's really low on my list."

"It's high on a trauma surgeon's list," I replied. "Can't mess with the quota."

She frowned, set her hands on her hips and slowly shook his head. "And he's back."

I frowned in return.

"Jeff took your patients yesterday so you're not double booked. However, you've got a patient in room one and Mrs. Krase is up next, so be prepared."

I nodded. "Yes, ma'am."

"Oh, Mac called about lunch again today. It seems he's smitten with you. I told him you can't because of patient appointments but you're free at four for happy hour."

"I appreciate you scheduling my social life."

"Your calendar shows you booked every day at six, so I figure four would work."

I looked down at the industrial carpet and adjusted the stethoscope and tried not to smile. I wasn't planning on telling her what happened every day at *sex* o'clock.

53

MALLORY

I WAS BEING SILLY. Like a sixteen-year-old, but I didn't care. I felt like I needed an excuse to see Theo but delivering him his jacket he'd forgotten at Lindy's house this morning was flimsy. I was content with flimsy.

Maybe it was because I was in a good mood. I was back in Hunter Valley a free woman. I was getting sex on the regular. This morning in the shower with Theo had been a first. When he said he loved pussy, he hadn't been joking.

Right now, my clit throbbed with eagerness for more of his mouth.

I entered the doctor's office, Theo's coat tucked under my arm.

"–book every day at six, so I figure four would work." Verna was standing in the open office doorway, her back to me.

"Thanks." That was Theo who responded.

Verna must've heard the door because she stuck her head out, saw me, then turned back to Theo. "I assume Mallory Mornay's your six o'clock?"

I stilled, confused why she was talking about me with Theo when she knew I was standing right here.

"How do you know that?" Theo replied. I could hear the surprise in his voice. I'd known Verna a long time. She knew everything about everyone. It amazed me that Theo hadn't caught on to that yet.

"That smile," she said to him.

I blushed, then looked around, wondering if I should hear this. I should. Since Verna knew I was here, but clearly not Theo, their conversation was fair game.

And I wanted to know about the smile he had on his face.

"I'm not smiling because of Mallory."

I clenched his puffy jacket and barely breathed.

"Oh? Gas pains?"

"Verna," Theo warned.

"I thought you and Mallory had a thing going on."

"How do you know that?"

She didn't say anything because I assumed she was giving him a look.

"There is no thing," he replied.

What?

"Oh? Then what is it?"

"There are some things a gentleman doesn't share."

"I'm not talking about that. I'm talking about love."

Theo laughed. "Love? I don't love Mallory Mornay. It's just a standing–" He cleared his throat.

"Are you stringing her along then?" Verna sounded pissed.

I was too stunned to be pissed. I'm just a standing... yeah, I could fill in that blank.

"Of course not. Mallory knows that it's only... you know."

"Because Tom Zajik had chlamydia and you didn't want her to get it on their date."

WHAT? My mouth fell open and I leaned against the wall because... wow.

That was why Theo had been at The Lodge. That was why Tom had fled. Not diarrhea. That was why Theo had stepped in to have sex with me. Because the only guy who'd want me slept around and picked up sexually transmitted diseases.

"We don't talk about patients, Verna," Theo warned.

"I heard it from Sandra Nimoy, the gym teacher at the high school. I was in line behind her at the grocery store. I said hello and she told me all about it. It's definitely not a secret."

Everyone knew about Tom but me.

But that wasn't important because Theo knew. He just inferred he was a patient.

"I'm talking about you and Mallory."

"Why are we talking about me and Mallory? There's nothing to say. There's just... nothing."

Nothing. I was nothing. I meant nothing to him. After everything we did together, that's what he felt. Nothing.

I bit my lip. God, fuck. Shit. Dammit! Was I lovable for anyone?

Now I was pissed.

I stomped over to Verna, who wisely stepped out of the way.

Theo's eyes widened. Clearly, he was surprised to see me. I tossed the coat at him. He caught it. "Mallory."

"Theo," I said. I was sure Theo could give some sort of wordy explanation for the adrenaline dump I just had. My body was shaking. My heart was pounding. "I wanted sex. I made that very clear. It was understood. You definitely gave it to me."

"Mallory–"

I held up my hand and pushed on. "You didn't offer anything more. You set no false expectations."

Fuck, was I glad I gave him the house back. Yeah, fuck. Not fudge. Screw fudge and sugar and all the stupid swear word alternatives.

"Just sex. I think I've had a thorough education now and you've done your job. So thank you."

"Mallory," he said, his eyes narrowing in anger.

Why the hell would he be angry?

"It's not like that."

I nodded. "It is. It's nothing, remember?"

Those words hurt to come out, but I had to do it. I couldn't linger where I wasn't wanted.

"See you around."

I spun on my heel, faced Verna. Her eyes held sympathy, but she tipped her chin up. I tipped mine up in return. I knew, silently, she'd started that conversation for me and was telling me to be strong.

I could do that. I could take care of myself. I always had.

54

THEO

"What was that, Verna?" I asked, gripping my coat. I followed after her into the waiting room. Mallory was long gone.

She tipped her head, gave me a look I expected any mother with teenagers had perfected.

"You knew she was there?"

"That girl needs a man who's going to stick."

"I stick."

She pursed her lips as she settled behind the counter. "More like you stick it in her."

My mouth opened and I stared at her. "I can't believe you just said that."

She raised her arm and pointed toward the front door. "You think I don't know what you've been up to?"

Silas knew. Bridget and Mav knew. Of course Verna knew.

"I've known Mallory her entire life. Sweet as can be, even with her crazy parents. I will not stand by and let you use her."

"I'm not using her," I countered. "It's... mutual."

Again, with the look.

"I bought her a house."

Her eyes widened. "You did what?"

"I bought her a house."

"She wanted it?"

"The house? Of course. It's the one she's been eyeing."

Verna shook her head. "I meant, did she want it from you?"

"She wasn't... happy."

Verna humphed. "That's what I thought."

I ran a hand through my hair. "What does that mean?"

"She doesn't want a house. She wants love."

I held up my hands. Stepped back. "Not happening from me. I don't do love. I can't."

Verna shrugged. "Then you were right. It's nothing."

I opened my mouth to say more, but she pointed again, this time toward room one. "You have a patient waiting."

55

MALLORY

THE DAY WAS TURNING to shit. Not only did I know how Theo really felt about me, that he truly was interested in me only for sex, but my mother texted. Again.

> I scraped together a little money for the mechanic since you wouldn't pay. Now we have no food. Send me money for groceries.

Gah.

I was so tired of people using me. I sat in my car outside of Lindy's house. The engine was still running, and I hadn't moved in five minutes. I'd tossed the trash from the road trip earlier, but there were chip crumbs all over the place. I could even smell a hint of Theo's spicy cologne. The fucker.

No. No, I couldn't be mad at Theo. It wasn't his fault my heart got involved. As I told him, he'd set no false expectations. Never lied. He was always up front with me. Up until last night, we hadn't even spent the night in the same bed. It had *always* been about sex.

It was my own stupid heart all over again thinking someone would actually care about me deep down. That I was more to them than a money machine, or a sex machine.

I wanted what Bridget and Mav had. God, their connection was insane. Same went for Dex and–

My phone rang.

"I was just thinking about you," I said.

Lindy laughed. The love Dex had for her was what I wanted–no, I deserved–from a man. I was the one Dex told first that he was going to marry Lindy. I even went ring shopping with him. He fell first and he fell hard. He hadn't wavered. Not once, all the while Lindy got her head on right and finally fell for him.

I wanted that same unwavering devotion.

"Well, I hope it's something good," she replied.

"It is. Thanks again for letting me stay at the house. I promise I won't be there too long."

"Yes, the house."

"Uh oh." I recognized that tone of voice, like I was in trouble. Visions of seventh grade and Bridge and I cutting each other's bangs came to mind.

"Yeah, uh oh. Why is it that there was an emergency call for someone being murdered at the house?"

"No one was being murdered," I told her.

I flushed hotly, remembering that embarrassing situation.

"Oh, I know. I got the truth from Hunter. It is my house and all."

I closed my eyes and groaned.

"I think it's great, you and Theo."

"There is no me and Theo," I told her.

"Oh? Were you actually trying to murder him then? I thought–"

"Thoughts are dangerous, Lind."

"Oh."

"Yeah, oh."

"You care about him, don't you?"

Hearing Lindy's soft voice asking me that almost broke me. She cared. She only wanted what was best for me, what made me happy. But while I was thankful for that, I wanted that devotion to come from Cheryl. Even from Theo.

Lindy was just a love tease, in that I knew what it should be like, but it wasn't coming from someone who was supposed to offer it unconditionally, or someone who wanted me to belong to him unconditionally.

"Yes, but I did it to myself. I assumed he'd feel things for me in return. I should've known better."

"Hey," she warned.

"I know. I know. Cheryl's a piece of work and a waste of my time."

"Right."

"She just asked for money."

"I'm not going to say *again?*" She sighed. "Are you going to give it to her?"

I shook my head, even though she couldn't see it. "No. I'm going to take her to the store and buy her groceries. Ensure that's what she's really doing with the cash."

"Mal–"

"I've got to go. I want to deal with her and get back. That new bathtub of yours has jets that are calling my name."

I ended the call with Lindy and put my car into gear.

Ten minutes later, I was pulling up in front of my parents' house. I'd deal with my mother. Get it over with.

56

THEO

I DROPPED into a chair across from Mac. He wasn't alone, but with the entire engine crew. All six of them were decked out in their navy fire uniforms and eating burgers and wings. A row of walkie talkies were on the tables, a reminder that while they were having a meal, they were always on call. The fire truck positioned around the corner for easy response couldn't be missed either.

"You look like when we first met," he said, shoving a fry in his mouth.

"How's that?" I asked, tipping my chin in greeting to the others. They didn't say much, just shoveled in their meals. I wondered what they'd been up to before this to want all those calories.

"Like you've got a stick up your ass again," he said.

I frowned. "Early dinner?"

He picked up his own burger, took a huge bite, then spoke with his mouth full. "We eat when it's quiet. Never know when we'll get a call."

The waitress came over and I pointed at Mac's burger. "I'll have one of those, please."

With greasy fingers, he pushed a large envelope across the table. "This is for you."

I picked it up, studied the label. It had my name on it with Hunter Valley Clerk and Recorder Office at the top. "How'd you get this?"

"Mary, who works at city hall, knows you and I are friends. Asked if I knew your address."

"Jesus, small town life. She could have called Verna. She knows everything." *As she keeps reminding me.*

"She did. Said Verna was mad at you."

I humphed.

He eyed me, then wiped his mouth and mustache with a napkin. "Anyway, I told Mary I was seeing you and she passed this on to give you."

I frowned at the envelope as I opened it, pulled out the single piece of paper.

"What is it?" he asked, taking another bite.

"It's–" Holy fuck. "It's a deed to a house." To Mallory's house. The one I gave her. And the one she obviously gave back. She couldn't have done that in the past two hours since she overheard my conversation with Verna. I scanned the copy of the Quit Claim Deed again, noticed the date. Yesterday.

Which meant it had been filed and recorded while we were driving back from Vegas. Which meant she'd done the paperwork before then.

"She gave it back to me right after she got it," I said absently.

57

MALLORY

"You could've just given me the money. Saved both of us some time," Cheryl said, her words laced with attitude. She was in the passenger seat, arms crossed. Angry. I wondered who was the parent and who was the child.

Because I didn't trust her, I checked her fridge, saw that it was empty, as she said. She then held out her hand as if I'd pull a wad of cash from my wallet and hand it over. Instead, I told her if she wanted groceries, we'd be going shopping together. I wanted to ensure the money went to actual food and staples, not cigarettes or liquor.

Now we were on the way to the store, a fifteen-minute ride back into town from the foothills where they lived. My dad was left behind, in his recliner with a late afternoon talk show on the TV. He'd turned away from the programming and his beer long enough to say hi.

"Probably," I replied. "Why are you short again?"

She huffed, then looked at me. The waft of liquor came from her breath. I didn't turn my head from the road but winced at the odor that mixed with the smoke clinging to her clothes.

"Because you didn't pay to have the car fixed."

"Neither did you, from your text. Only a small portion."

"Well," she began, grabbing her purse by her feet. She pulled out her pack of cigarettes.

"No smoking," I said.

Another huff and she put them back.

"Well?" I prompted.

"I quit my job."

I blinked, death gripped the steering wheel, then took a deep breath. "Why? Was your boss handsy like the last one?"

I wasn't for asshole employers, but in Cheryl's case, frequently when she quit over the years, she pulled out that excuse. Now I was never sure if she cried wolf or not.

"No. I won at nickel slots at the casino on the reservation."

I glanced her way for a second, then back on the road, slowing for a curve. "You gambled? While you don't have money and make me pay your rent and car repair bills?"

She waved her hand. "I won ten thousand dollars so I didn't need that job any longer."

I was stunned. That was a lot of money for playing the slots.

"Then why am I taking you to get groceries?"

"I told you you didn't have to. I'd be at home right now with my drinky-poo and you'd be off living your life like you always do."

"No, you told me to just give you money," I said, diplomatically as possible. "Why do you need it from me if you made ten thousand dollars? That will pay the car bill, plus your rent and groceries for the next six months."

"Because I lost it all."

I slowed, then pulled off onto the shoulder. Now I could give Cheryl my complete attention because I thought she said she lost it all. "You *lost* it all?"

She nodded. Her blonde hair, which used to be the same shade as mine, was in need of a root touchup and gray coverage. Between her drinking and smoking, she was weathered and rough looking for her age. I had to wonder how sober she was right now, especially if she wasn't working.

I remembered when she was beautiful, but she'd always been mean spirited. Self-centered.

"I lost it playing craps."

"You gambled away all *ten thousand dollars?*"

"The table was hot! Then some bitch in high heels blew on the dice and the luck changed."

I stared at her wide eyed. She was serious.

"You're blaming your loss of all that money on a bitch in high heels? It's not her fault! It's yours!"

"The table was hot until she walked up."

"Oh my fucking God!" I flung my arms in the air. Somehow, for some reason, right now, sitting on the side of the road, I was done. D.O.N.E. Done. "That's it. I'm out."

I turned to face the road, looked over my shoulder to see if a car was coming, then pulled out. She grabbed my arm. "Out? Out of what?"

I headed back toward her house.

"Out of taking care of you. Of wasting my time, my money, my emotions on you."

"Don't be silly, I'm your mother."

I stepped on the gas, driving faster so I could get rid of her sooner. Like Arlo said, I should have done this years ago. She would never love me. I'd been hoping for scraps of affection even when, deep down, I knew it would never come. Why had I seen it so fast with Theo, but not with her? It didn't matter. I was done with him. I was done with her. I deserved being loved completely.

"I'm dropping you off at home and you will not call me. You will not stop by. You will not get in touch with me in any way."

"What?" she grabbed my arm in a talon-like grip. "I need you."

I shook my head. "No, you don't. You're an ungrateful, mean woman. If you want to be my mother, then act like one. Until then, we're done."

"Oh, it's Lindy Beckett's influence that you're talking to me like this."

I smiled then, thought of my call with her just a little while ago.

I glanced at Cheryl and said, "Yes, it is."

Then the screech of tires had me jerking my head back to the road in front of me, but it was too late.

The impact was instantaneous, then the world went black.

58

THEO

THE WAITRESS CAME BY, sat a glass of ice water on a coaster in front of me.

"She gave *what* back to you?" Mac asked.

"Mallory. I bought her a house and she returned it. Like a pair of socks she bought in the wrong size at the store," I explained on a grumble.

Mac's mouth opened and a piece of bun fell out and onto his plate. "You bought Mallory a house?"

I nodded.

He grinned. "Congrats!"

I frowned again. "Why?"

"Because she's great and you need someone who's all sunshiny for your grumpy ass."

"We're not together."

He frowned. "I know I'm divorced and all which makes me a shit judge of relationships, but what the fuck?"

"It's just sex."

The walkie talkies chimed all at once. The crew stood, their chairs scraping across the floor in their haste. Food was set down, radios picked up and the crew practically ran out of the place. Patrons turned to watch as they left. Mac stood but hadn't moved, listening to the dispatcher give the report of the call.

"MVA, mile marker twenty-six on Highway 5. Head on, car versus truck, multiple injuries."

Mac looked to me, his gaze laser sharp. "You're coming along. We're going to need all the help we can get."

I hopped up, the familiar hum of an emergency coursing through my veins.

Mac turned to leave and waved to Arlo. He gave a nod and a wave in reply as I followed Mac out onto the street. I assumed that meant they'd settle up for their meals later.

The fire engine was running with the back door open, ready for Mac to hop in. And me.

I followed him in, and I had the door barely closed before the sirens kicked on and we were headed out of town.

Mac slipped on a headset, and I found one at my side and did the same. I could hear dispatch and the crew in my ears. I put on my shoulder harness and listened to the reports coming in from the scene, seconds apart.

"Three injuries."

"Pickup truck versus small SUV."

"Older model black Ford F-150 and a white Honda CRV."

"People stopping to help say two women are unconscious. Unknown if breathing. Trapped."

I looked to Mac. Over his head, he grabbed a box of gloves and tossed it to me. "Put a bunch of those in your pocket. We'll have our med kits for you to use but be ready. If they're trapped, it'll be like the practice we did with you. Jaws of Life, whatever's needed."

"I didn't see shit under that blanket," I said as I tugged on the gloves.

"You'll be on the other side of an emergency again. You good?"

I frowned. "Why wouldn't I be?" The shrill siren was muted by the headphones, but it was a constant reminder that lives were at stake. This wasn't the ER or the OR. This was truly life or death. There were only so many supplies, only so much that could be done on the side of the road. Even for me, who had a medical degree and tackled traumas day in and day out.

"Because shit's about to get real."

I glanced at the rest of the crew in the back. Three others were already geared up and ready to go.

"It's always real," I said.

"These are people, fucker."

I shook my head. "These are victims. We treat them, get them back to their lives."

The engine slowed and I leaned to the side to see out the window. It turned as it came to a stop, angled so the entire street was blocked, protecting the crew from anyone crazy enough to drive into an accident scene. The crew hopped from the door on the opposite side as I looked out the window. Mac shifted to move, but I grabbed his arm. Pointed.

"That CRV is Mallory's." The one that was upside down

and half under the pickup truck and wedged into the guardrail.

I recognized the sticker on the back windshield, which was shattered.

He looked to me, then at the car out the window.

His face went blank. Intense. "Let's get to work."

I followed him, hopping down from the high seats. His crew had split up to assess the situation. One was standing in the open door of the truck, talking to the driver. Another handed off an oxygen mask and they put it over his mouth and nose. One victim was conscious and breathing.

Another firefighter was kneeling on the ground at the back of the CRV, checking for stability since it was upside down. Two others were testing the doors and trying to figure out how to gain access. It was clear the driver door was crushed in. It wasn't in as bad of shape as the practice car I'd crawled into in the back lot of the fire station, but it was close.

Mac went toward the CRV. I followed but he held me back with his arm.

"You don't have the gear to get any closer. We need to brace the car, then get them out."

Shattered glass and flung car parts were strewn across the road. Something was leaking and creeping downhill.

"Is she in there?" I asked, suddenly freaking out.

"It doesn't matter *who* is in there. Whoever it is needs our help."

What? It doesn't matter? It could be Mallory. MALLORY.

When Mac turned around to start working on the CRV

and get the people out–whoever they were–it hit me. Like a big, old F150 on a curving stretch of road.

I felt.

I felt fear.

I felt anger.

I felt helplessness.

I felt worry.

I felt *everything* because inside that car was Mallory.

The woman who seemed to like me despite the stick up my ass. Despite the fact that I'd never been on a road trip. Or that I had a plane. That I slotted her into my calendar as a daily appointment. I remembered calling patients a quota. That Bridge had kicked me out of her classroom because I couldn't see why I went to the high school to ask after Mallory.

I did have a stick up my ass. No wonder everyone rolled their eyes at me. Or gave me a look of disappointment. I was one. A big fucking doofus, like Bridge said.

Mac squatted down by the window, peeked in. He turned, looked at me and nodded. I *felt* because Mallory was inside the destroyed car, and I didn't know if she was alive or dead.

Mallory, the woman who'd been mine all along and I never knew it.

59

THEO

I RAN OVER, grabbed the Pulaski took from a firefighter before he could give it to Mac.

"What are you doing?" Mac shouted.

"Mallory's in there!"

Mac grabbed the ax from me and passed it off, then shoved me out of the way. "Get your shit together. It's our job to get the patients out. You don't have the gear or the skill. Get your head on straight."

I wanted to punch him, but he was right.

The firefighter–I wasn't paying any attention to who it was–worked the tool into the seam between the driver door and the frame, right by the pin. Another firefighter used his booted foot to kick in the shattered windshield. Another two were doing the same on the other side. All wore thick bunker gear, heavy leather gloves, helmets, and even protective goggles.

I had on latex gloves.

Police cars pulled up along with another fire truck.

A whistle pierced the air and I turned to follow the sound. "Doc, over here!"

I glanced at Mallory's car again.

"Go do your job." Mac slapped me on the shoulder, then turned away from me to get to work.

Fuck. FUCK!

Mallory was in that car, and I had to walk away. I had to get my shit together, had to triage, and that meant going where I was called and assessing. I had to wait to help Mallory and whoever else was in the CRV.

I ran over to the firefighter helping the man in the truck. "Fifty-three, wearing his seat belt. BP is one forty over ninety, resps are ninety. Complaining of upper chest pain, most likely a broken clavicle due to seat belt. No allergies to medicines, no drugs or alcohol usage."

The EMT gave me a thorough report as I assessed the man.

"Pen light?"

The EMT handed me one from the med kit and I flashed it back and forth in front of his face. "What's your name, sir?"

He pulled the oxygen mask back to answer. "Donald Naimar."

"Did you hit your head on the steering wheel or windshield?" I asked, feeling his skull as I took in that his car had no airbag.

"No."

"Doc, I'll take over here." I turned and there was one of the paramedics from the Saturday training. "One patient's about to be pulled from the car and you'll be needed."

"Donald, you're in good hands with these guys."

I gave him a quick but reassuring smile before I ran for the car, stripping my gloves as I went. I pulled new ones from my pocket–Mac was fucking smart–and saw that it was the passenger who was being placed on a backboard.

"Careful! Grab my purse. I need my cigarettes if you're taking me in an ambulance." That was not Mallory.

"Ma'am, please remain as still as possible. You've been in a car accident, and we don't know the extent of your injuries."

"I don't hurt. Nothing hurts," she replied as I made it around the car and squatted down beside her laying on the backboard. I gave her a quick assessment. C-collar on. Conscious, therefore her heart was beating, and she was breathing. Her airway was very clear, and she smelled like a liquor cabinet.

"What's your name, ma'am?"

"Cheryl."

"Cheryl, who's driving the car?"

I peeked in the open doorway, tilting my body to see in. Cheryl said, "My daughter. Mallory," at the same time I saw her.

Mallory was unconscious, caught in her seatbelt and dangling upside down. Blood dripped from a cut on her temple onto the deflated airbag.

I was pushed out of the way so another rescuer could get into the passenger spot.

I looked to the two EMTs adjusting the straps on the board and placing an oxygen mask over her face.

"She and the man in the truck are both Level 4. Get them both to the ER pronto."

"On it, Doc."

I stood, backed up to let the crew work. Cheryl, Mallory's miserable–and clearly intoxicated–mother was carted off. Not once did she ask after her daughter.

"Breathing!" the woman half in-half out of the upside-down car called.

I sighed, closed my eyes.

I thought of the boy who'd died on my operating table. The one who'd been in a car accident like this one. Who'd been ejected and died.

I didn't even remember his name.

He was the reason I'd moved to Hunter Valley. Because I'd been numb. Uncaring.

I'd thought quitting and relocating would have changed me.

It didn't.

Mallory did.

She'd made me see the fun side of things. She was the one who struggled. Suffered. Hurt. Ached. Bled. And I'd never understood. I'd disregarded her feelings, her words. I'd diminished her.

I made her... oh fuck. *Nothing.*

That's what I told Verna earlier. That we were nothing.

I grabbed my hair. I made her feel like nothing when she was *everything.*

"Come on! What's taking so long?" I shouted.

No one paid me any attention. Everyone was busy doing their jobs and I was standing around with my thumb up my ass.

"C-collar on. Board!"

A backboard was produced and worked into the car through the open passenger door. The straps were rolled up at the sides, ready.

"Cutting the seatbelt on three." It was Mac calling from the other side. "One. Two. Three!"

Everyone shifted, and I couldn't see a fucking thing.

Five, then ten seconds passed and then the board was slid out.

"Doc!"

I ran over, dropped to my knees.

"O2. Vitals. Get her strapped down and I want her out of here in thirty. I'll assess on the way to the ER."

I ran my hands over her as the straps were put across her, securing her to the board. I lifted the hem of her shirt– the one I recognized her wearing earlier–to look for signs of bruising, felt for possible internal bleeding.

"Ready."

I stood and moved back out of the way.

"On three." The firefighters hoisted her in unison and hustled her to the back of the waiting ambulance.

I slid onto the bench beside her, the paramedic at my side. Mac stood between the open back doors, and he gave me a smile. I tipped my chin, then he slammed the doors shut. I heard the slap on the side of the rig and we were off.

I was back in trauma surgeon mode, and this was one patient whose name I knew.

She wouldn't be a fucking quota, like I told Verna. She was mine. I was going to make her mine, tell her what she meant to me. How much of a dumbass I was.

If she lived.

60

MALLORY

I woke up to beeping. And the strong smell of cleaning supplies. And a wicked headache.

"Easy."

I blinked my eyes open, turned toward the voice. The one I recognized and was oh-so-soft. Like a gentle whisper.

I felt a hand in mine, a thumb brushing over my palm.

"Theo."

He sat beside the bed, leaning toward me. His gaze raked over my face, but I didn't see any of his usual tenseness. Or anger. Or lust. Or any other emotion I was used to from him.

Now, all I saw was tenderness.

"There's my tiger. I've been waiting for you to wake up."

"What... what happened?" I was in a hospital room, hooked up to monitors and an IV.

"What do you remember?"

I closed my eyes, thought back. "Oh. There was an accident."

"Yes."

I turned my head, looked to Theo, whose eyes seemed haunted. I'd never seen him look this way before. "I hit someone."

He shook his head. "Someone hit you. Took a curve too wide."

"Are they okay?"

He offered a small smile. "Yes. He's got a broken collar bone, but he's on good pain meds and is happily letting his wife take care of him."

"And Cheryl?" We'd been arguing. I'd been so angry I'd turned around to take her home. To literally get rid of her.

He clenched his jaw and gave my hand a gentle squeeze. "Not a scratch on her."

Of course not. "She'd been drinking."

Theo nodded. "Yes. Intoxicated people have slow reaction times. They don't tense up before an accident. Helps them from getting hurt."

"Is she–"

"Hunter, you remember him?" Theo arched a brow and gave me a soft smile. Yeah, a smile. "He took her home."

So she wasn't here at the hospital waiting for me to wake up. I didn't ask if she worried about me. I didn't want to know. I made it clear she was out of my life now and I meant it. The fact that she'd left...

"What are you doing here?" I asked. It didn't make any sense why he might be by my bedside holding my hand.

"I was with Mac when the call came in. I was there when they pulled you out of the car."

I frowned. "Was I operated on?" I didn't feel hurt other than a headache.

"No. I checked you over in the back of the ambulance, then handed you off to the ER team. Do you have a headache?" he wondered.

It pulsed. Throbbed. Ached. Like I'd gone through a blender. "Yeah."

"You hit the airbag pretty hard, then something else when the car flipped."

"The car flipped?" I had no idea.

Theo looked grim. Bleak even.

"Now that you're awake, you'll be checked for a concussion, but it's pretty much a given," he explained.

"Thank you," I said.

"You're awake!" Bridget said, coming into the room.

"Shh," I said.

Mav followed behind her but remained quiet.

"You scared the shit out of me," Bridge whispered, leaning in to give me a gentle hug. She took in Theo holding my hand but said nothing about it.

I didn't know what it meant and I was too out of it to process.

"Well, the doctor says you're spending the night for observation, then you're staying with me for a few days."

I swallowed, but my mouth was so dry. "I'm not staying at your house. You guys have too much sex."

"Fine, then I'll stay with you at the house. It'll be like a sleepover when we were kids. Lindy heard about the accident and is on her way."

I glanced at Theo, remembering the last sleepover I had there with him. No more though. I was thankful he'd been there to help, but his medical skills–or any other talents he had–weren't needed any longer. "Thanks again, Theo. I'll... see you around."

He was a doctor, and he was checking on a patient. It was required. He'd made an oath or something. He'd looked after Cheryl, too.

I was fine or would be. Bridge was here and she was going to mother the hell out of me. Lindy, too.

After what I went through with Cheryl, it sounded great.

"Mallory, I..." Theo said.

"I'm good. Thanks for doctoring me."

Realizing he was dismissed–it wasn't like we were anything since he made that crystal clear–he stood. "Right. Um... bye."

I watched him leave and wondered if I was ever going to get over him. While he felt nothing for me, I felt so much. I wondered if it was more than my head splitting in two. It felt like my heart was too.

61

THEO

I STARTLED awake when I felt breathing on my neck. I turned my head and got a whiff of dog breath, then got a tongue lick.

"Fuck, Scout," I said, wiping my face. He jumped to the floor and barked.

"Good, you're not dead," Mav said.

I blinked my eyes open, and he loomed over me, arms crossed over his chest.

"What time is it?"

"Two-thirty."

I shifted, realized I was on the couch and in the clothes I had on yesterday. The inside of my mouth felt like the floor of a mushroom farm.

"Mac was expecting you at the fire training six hours ago."

"Yeah, well, I didn't go."

Mav sighed. "Look. I'm all for you taking a bender. If anyone needs one, it's you. But your shit is fucking with my sex life."

I sat up, then regretted it. I held my head so it didn't fall off. I wasn't sure how far I made it through the whiskey bottle last night but based on the way I wanted to hurl and then die, it was probably at least half.

"How am I fucking with your sex life?"

"Because Bridge has stayed the past three nights at her house with Mal instead of in my bed."

That meant it was Saturday. I spent Thursday and Friday sober, doing my job and seeing patients. Verna hadn't said a word to me outside of work-related topics. Jeff just gave me pitying looks. When I was done for the week, when I didn't have to be a functioning–and sober–member of society, I came home and got plastered.

Now that I was conscious again, I realized it hadn't helped.

I still felt like shit.

Mallory still wasn't mine.

"Shower and then we'll figure this shit out."

Standing, I groaned. After stumbling to the bathroom, I threw up, getting rid of all the stuff my body didn't like, just like I'd told the group of first graders. Only when my stomach was blissfully empty did I swallow a few pain pills, then stand under the hot water until my skin pruned.

Surprisingly, Mav was still in my house when I came out in sweats and a t-shirt. The scent of bacon and eggs made my stomach flip, but the cup of coffee Mav handed to me calmed it. I ignored how it scalded my tongue and drank it all.

"Here." A plate of food was held in front of me. I snagged it, then gave my brother a look.

"You have no sympathy."

"You brought this shit on yourself. You could be with Mal right now. Instead, we're both suffering."

"Oh yeah, your poor dick." I picked up the fork and shoveled in a mouthful of eggs.

"My dick shouldn't be in the middle of your love life."

I glowered, then ate some more.

"Let me guess, you pulled your head out of your ass and figured out you're in love with Mal."

"Pretty much." I clenched my teeth around a piece of bacon and ripped it in half.

Scout and the stray cat sat side-by-side staring up at me.

"What's the cat doing inside?"

Mav shrugged. "Followed Scout in."

I ripped the remaining piece of bacon in half and gave it to each of them. Scout didn't even chew his. The cat set it on the floor, sniffed it, then ate it daintily.

I was impressed Scout didn't try to steal it.

"So. You're in love with Mal and she's with Bridge. Let's get this figured out."

"I feel like you're here for selfish reasons and not for brotherly ones."

I finished the food, rinsed the dish and put it in the dishwasher.

"Purely selfish."

I grabbed a glass from the cabinet, filled it at the sink and downed the whole thing. I was starting to feel slightly human. Except I also felt... empty.

"I was with Mac when they got the call. I got pulled

along and it turned out to be Mallory in the car." I'd never forget that moment. "I was helpless. All my training to be a doctor and I couldn't help. Mac and his crew got her out."

"So you had to stand there and realize that you actually have emotions after all."

I nodded. "The kid who was killed, the one I told you about?"

"Yeah?" He leaned against the counter and crossed his ankles.

"I felt nothing. Then... when I was waiting to find out if Mallory was dead or alive, I felt *everything.* Panic. Fear. God, the fear."

"Welcome to loving someone."

"It's too late. I was talking to Verna and Mallory overheard me say we were nothing."

His eyes widened, but he stayed quiet.

"It was just supposed to be sex. It *was* just sex."

"Until it wasn't," he added. "Congratulations, you're human, not a cyborg."

"Funny." I didn't laugh. "But probably really fucking accurate. We had a scheduled time for sex. No lingering. Hell, we didn't even kiss for a few days. And only because she pointed it out, that she wanted a connection. Me? I was fine with just going at it." I glanced at Mav, felt the gravity of what I'd done settle in. "I'm Dad."

Mav laughed. "Hell, no."

"I am. I can fuck without caring about a woman. I *bought* Mallory a house because it would solve her problems."

"From what I understand, you confronted Mr. Dirty Dick–Bridge's name for the guy she works with–to keep

Mal safe. You bought her a house because, like you said, it solves her problems. You flew to Vegas because you heard she had a court appearance and had driven her ass there all by herself."

"You know about the court appearance?" I asked, surprised.

He raised a hand. "Oh, I learned a fuckton in the past few days. I didn't think Mal had it in her to get arrested for solicitation, but I think I'm actually a little proud of her."

"What are you getting at?" He had to have a point.

"In your own cyborg way, you were showing her how much you cared about her. You felt for her all along. You just needed that heart thawed out."

"Mav, she gave the house back. She Quit Claimed the deed into my name."

His eyes widened in surprise.

"She wanted that place so fucking bad, but she didn't want it from me."

He shook his head. "You gave her the wrong thing, dumbass."

I paused, considered. For the first time, it was obvious. "You're talking about my heart."

"Yes, you moron. She wants *you*. For some reason, the women we fall for don't give a shit about our money."

"Clearly they want our dicks," I replied.

Mav smiled, then frowned, because he wasn't getting any.

"Buying a house for a woman is a Dad move. I wonder how many gifts he bought for the women he fucked and forgot."

"No more of this *you're like Dad* bullshit. If you're like

him, then I am, too. I got me a girl who's fifteen years younger. I pretty much robbed the cradle. If that isn't just like the fucker, I don't know what is."

"Fucking without feeling," I said. "Then giving her a house. Hell, she must've felt like a real call girl. The best BJ of my life and I buy her a house."

He grimaced but pushed on. "You have feelings, you idiot. You like Mac. From what I hear you two are BFFs. I don't see you buying him a house."

"Not too keen on him giving me a BJ," I countered, trying to be funny. It wasn't.

"You just buried all your shit down so you didn't get hurt. Dad was a narcissist and used people. He didn't give a shit about their feelings or emotions. He wouldn't have become a doctor to *save* people like you did. You forgot to have fun, that's all."

Fun. Fuck, there was that word again.

He was right. All of it. I wasn't telling him that.

"Since when do we talk feelings?" I wondered.

"Since my dick hasn't seen Bridge's pussy in three days."

I shook my head. "Dude. Please."

"No, dude, *please*." He begged me right back.

"Fine. Fine. I'll go grovel to Mallory to make your dick happy."

He held up a hand to stop me. "No. Absolutely not. The only reason to grovel to Mal is if you love her and want her to be yours. Long term. No scheduled sex. No whatever other stupid parameters you put around your heart. You gotta be all in. Or walk away for good."

62

MALLORY

I DIDN'T WORK the rest of last week after the accident. Today, Monday, was my first day back. I was tired but feeling better. If sad and depressed and droopy was feeling better.

I came out of school, expecting Bridge to be waiting to pick me up. I'd texted her a half hour ago to give her a heads up on when I would be done. My car had been totalled and I hadn't finalized the insurance paperwork to get a replacement.

It wasn't Bridge though, but Theo.

I pulled my coat closer around me as I went over to him. He was leaning against his car door, patient as ever. As handsome as ever, too. His beard was trimmed so he didn't look too unruly, giving a balance to his doctor persona and his new small town life.

"What are you doing here?" I asked. I tried to keep my

heart from beating out of my chest–to try to get to him–but it was hard. He looked good, as if he was a piece of cake I hadn't had in a while but knew was delicious.

"To give you a ride home."

"Is Bridge okay?"

He nodded. "She's fine."

"She's in trouble," I muttered.

He shook his head. "I'm the one in trouble, aren't I?"

I went around the car to the passenger side and he followed, opening it for me.

Climbing in, I set my bag on the floor at my feet.

Theo slid into the driver's seat and shut the door, cocooning us in quiet. And his scent.

"How are you feeling?" he asked, doing his body scan again. I felt heat wherever his gaze went.

"Fine. I slept most of the weekend. Just some bruises left."

"Headaches?"

I shook my head.

He grabbed three little leather balls and held them up. "I was going to juggle for you when you came out."

I couldn't help but smile. "You juggle?"

Nodding, the corner of his mouth tipped up. "Silas and I learned one summer. Thought we might go and join the circus and needed a talent."

My smile faded. "You mean run away."

"Yes."

"Because of your dad."

His eyes were on mine. He barely blinked, barely looked away. Just looked *into* me.

"Yes. He was never around. When he was, he used our

affection for him as a weapon. Critiqued everything we did. If we played soccer, we had to win. If we didn't win, we sucked. He told us that, then gave us the silent treatment. Silas and I picked up juggling and it was... fun."

"Fun?" I asked, smiling.

"Until he said that Silas was better than me. Made juggling a competition. My brother and I hated each other by the time the summer was up. My dad laughed and said we were failures, that we couldn't even really juggle."

"Oh, Theo," I said, aching for the young child who'd been cruelly used.

"Love was conditional, Mallory. He used it as a weapon. It was when I realized he'd used it to pit me against Silas, that I saw him for what he was. Then I shut down."

I swallowed hard, tried not to cry.

"Fun isn't fun for me because of what that bastard did. I got serious and stayed that way. I... maybe, went to med school just to see if, one last time, he might be proud of me."

I took his hand. I couldn't *not* touch him.

His gaze dropped to our joined hold.

"Medical school and residency is *not* fun. It's grueling and only made me more the way I am. It went on from there. Working, no life, not caring or feeling for patients. Being serious and closed off. I felt nothing."

His eyes lifted to mine. "Until you."

"Theo," I began, but he shook his head.

"I stopped your date because of Tom's... situation, but I really did it because I didn't want anyone to have you but me. I was possessive of you even then. When I heard you wanted to have sex, I... I got jealous. Crazy. You were mine, Mallory, even then in that paper gown."

My heart beat frantically.

"You think we had sex every day at six because I made you nothing more than an appointment, but I started thinking of it as..." He stopped talking and I could have sworn his ears turned pink.

"As what?"

"*Sex* o'clock."

I couldn't help but laugh. He smiled, but sheepishly. "I loved knowing I would have you every day, that it was guaranteed. That if you were penciled in, it wouldn't be yanked away."

"Oh," I breathed, starting to understand.

"I bought you the house and met you in Vegas because you were mine to take care of. It was my way of telling you how I felt about you."

I swallowed. "How... how do you feel about me?"

"I'm not saying this because Mav wants Bridget to go home and stop staying with you."

"Okaaaaayy."

"I... I think I love you, Mallory."

Happiness gushed from me. I couldn't help but smile, to feel... glowing. "You think?"

He shook his head, unsure. Awkward. Completely unlike him.

"I don't know what love feels like. I care for my brothers, of course, but this is different. I want you to be safe in a house that's yours. I don't want you to fret or worry or work shifts with your brother to try to pay for it."

"But I–"

"I know you want to pay your way and I love that about you." He laughed. "See, that word again?"

I grinned.

"I'm going to buy you things to make your life easier. Starting with a car, of course. Not because you can't do it, but because it's how I will show you I care and want you to be happy and safe. I'm going to offer you the plane because I have one. I'm going to be grumbly and cranky and hate yoga and people and only want to be a crazy uncle. But I want to do all those things with you because you make me, make life... fun."

Tears fell now. I couldn't stop them.

"I can't give you anything like that in return," I admitted. "Unless I take up prostitution. I seem to be quite skilled at that. The first BJ I give, I get a house," I replied playfully.

His eyes heated, narrowed and I wasn't sure if he was angry at what I said or turned on.

"I only want you. Just like you didn't want the house from me. I get it now. You wanted me, didn't you?"

I nodded.

"You have me, Mallory. If you'll take me."

"Don't you want to know how I feel about you?" I asked.

He studied my face, then frowned. "I do. I really do. I think I was just hoping for scraps of affection from you because that's what I expect."

I shook my head, cupped his jaw. "No. No, you should have more than scraps. You should have a woman's whole heart because you're deserving of it."

He set his hand on top of mine. "We have fucked up parents."

I nodded. "We leave them behind. We move forward. Together, because I think I love you too, Theo."

He pulled me in and kissed me then. And kissed me. And kissed me some more. There was tongue involved and roaming hands. And more kissing.

"No prostitution for you," he said finally. "I like you sweet and slutty. You can be my little whore anytime you want. I don't share."

Oh my. Theo, my dirty talker.

"Except with Mr. VanMeyer and the Hunter Valley Police Department," I reminded.

He groaned. "We're moving into the little house I bought you that you gave me. It's our house now and we're sharing it together. No Mr. VanMeyer, no police. Just you, me and–"

"*Sex* o'clock."

EPILOGUE

SILAS

WHAT WAS it with the women in Hunter Valley, Montana? Why were they all so gorgeous? I didn't dare think how pretty either of the Beckett sisters was. Mav and Dex would kill me and my body would be added to the latest concrete pour at the James Inn site. Mallory was also hot as fuck, but she was Theo's now. Besides, she was too fucking perky for me. And she worked with six-year-olds; I couldn't handle the possibility of glitter in my life.

There was one woman though. Really, only one who filled my thoughts and made my dick hard.

Her.

The one who I was tugging into the office at the bar.

"Tell me what you like," I said, shutting the door behind us and taking in every inch of her perfect body in the sexy dress. It wasn't overly revealing, which to me seemed sexier than too much skin.

Tanned and toned, I wanted to kiss, lick and discover every silky, scented inch of her body.

"Orgasms," she replied, glancing at the front of my jeans and the way my dick was thick and long and barely contained behind the zipper and button.

I smiled, loving a woman who knew what she wanted. "That's a given. What else?"

"A quickie." She looked to the door, indicating while it was closed, it could open at any time—we didn't have all night. "I need it. This."

Her breathing was ragged and a flush spread up her cheeks.

She did. And fuck, did I also.

"Another given."

"I... I want you in charge," she admitted. "I don't want to think for once."

I stepped close, ran a knuckle down her soft cheek. Her eyes flared. Yeah, she was right here with me.

"Mmm, sweetness, I love to be in charge."

I stepped back, tipped my chin up as my hands went to my jeans to let my dick out to play. "Lift the dress. Show me how wet your panties are."

She licked her lips, then did as ordered.

"Good girl. Time for a hard, quick fuck. You'll come for me, three times and I promise you won't remember your name after."

I was the boss. Always. And people did what I said. She'd come and when we were done, I'd make sure the only name she could think of was mine.

*For more of Silas's story, get **Man Splain!** He might be in charge, but discover the woman who will rule his world.*

BONUS CONTENT

Guess what? I've got some bonus content for you! Sign up for my mailing list. There will be special bonus content for some of my books, just for my subscribers. Signing up will let you hear about my next release as soon as it is out, too (and you get a free book...wow!)

As always...thanks for loving my books and the wild ride!

JOIN THE WAGON TRAIN!

If you're on Facebook, please join my closed group, the Wagon Train! Don't miss out on the giveaways and hot cowboys!

https://www.facebook.com/groups/vanessavalewagontrain/

GET A FREE BOOK!

Join my mailing list to be the first to know of new releases, free books, special prices and other author giveaways.

http://freeromanceread.com

ALSO BY VANESSA VALE

For the most up-to-date listing of my books:

vanessavalebooks.com

On A Manhunt

Man Hunt

Man Candy

Man Cave

Man Splain

Man Scape

The Billion Heirs

Scarred

Flawed

Broken

Alpha Mountain

Hero

Rebel

Warrior

Billionaire Ranch

North

South

East

West

Bachelor Auction

Teach Me The Ropes

Hand Me The Reins

Back In The Saddle

Wolf Ranch

Rough

Wild

Feral

Savage

Fierce

Ruthless

Two Marks

Untamed

Tempted

Desired

Enticed

More Than A Cowboy

Strong & Steady

Rough & Ready

Wild Mountain Men

Mountain Darkness

Mountain Delights

Mountain Desire

Mountain Danger

Grade-A Beefcakes

Sir Loin of Beef

T-Bone

Tri-Tip

Porterhouse

Skirt Steak

Small Town Romance

Montana Fire

Montana Ice

Montana Heat

Montana Wild

Montana Mine

Steele Ranch

Spurred

Wrangled

Tangled

Hitched

Lassoed

Bridgewater County

Ride Me Dirty

Claim Me Hard

Take Me Fast

Hold Me Close

Make Me Yours

Kiss Me Crazy

Mail Order Bride of Slate Springs

A Wanton Woman

A Wild Woman

A Wicked Woman

Bridgewater Ménage

Their Runaway Bride

Their Kidnapped Bride

Their Wayward Bride

Their Captivated Bride

Their Treasured Bride

Their Christmas Bride

Their Reluctant Bride

Their Stolen Bride

Their Brazen Bride

Their Rebellious Bride

Their Reckless Bride

Bridgewater Brides World

Lenox Ranch Cowboys

Cowboys & Kisses

Spurs & Satin

Reins & Ribbons

Brands & Bows

Lassos & Lace

Montana Men

The Lawman

The Cowboy

The Outlaw

Standalones

Relentless

All Mine & Mine To Take

Bride Pact

Rough Love

Twice As Delicious

Flirting With The Law

Mistletoe Marriage

Man Candy - A Coloring Book

ABOUT VANESSA VALE

A USA Today bestseller, Vanessa Vale writes tempting romance with unapologetic bad boys who don't just fall in love, they fall hard. Her books have sold over one million copies. She lives in the American West where she's always finding inspiration for her next story. While she's not as skilled at social media as her kids, she loves to interact with readers.

vanessavaleauthor.com

facebook.com/vanessavaleauthor

instagram.com/vanessa_vale_author

amazon.com/author/vanessavale

bookbub.com/profile/vanessa-vale

tiktok.com/@vanessavaleauthor

Printed in Great Britain
by Amazon

41683491R00198